DRAGONS
IN CHAINS

First printing, October 2013
Revised edition, February 2015

Dragons In Chains is a work of fiction. Names, places, and incidents are either products of the author's mind or used fictitiously.

ISBN: 978-0-9891210-5-7

Dragons In Chains

Lee French

Book 2 of the Maze Beset trilogy

Acknowledgments

For Liam, Jayce, Sam, and Paul. You know who you are.

Prologue – Maisie

Summer in Honolulu meant work, from morning to night. Maisie didn't mind. Though exhausting, her job was fun. At the moment, she sat with the other girls in the show, rubbing her feet and grabbing what rest she could in the half hour break between performances. Normally, she stayed in costume all day. After an incident during the last show, she wore only her bikini and leafy wrist- and ankle-bands, with flowers woven into her black hair.

"Maisie, what happened?" Dave, the stage manager, leaned in and scowled at her.

"Talk to Rob," she snapped.

"I did. He said you flubbed the sequence."

Her nostrils flared with irritation and she narrowed her eyes. "He's a damned liar. He missed a step and I tripped over him. That ass is just lucky I was able to recover without falling on my butt."

"I saw it," Linda confirmed, nodding. She'd been directly behind them both as part of the chorus. "It was Rob's fault."

"When you go back and tell him we said so," Maisie sneered, "you can let him know I'm still not going to sleep with him, no matter how many times he asks."

Dave rolled his eyes. "You guys need to keep the personal stuff off the stage."

"Tell him, not me." Maisie stood up and jabbed a finger in the air. "I don't want any 'personal stuff' with him. Just because he gets to grab my ass on stage doesn't mean he gets access to it any other time."

Dave shook his head and huffed the sigh of a man who doesn't care but has to deal with it anyway. "You're not making my life any easier."

"I'm not the one causing a problem, Dave, he is." She held up her grass skirt so he could see the damage to the side. Two inches of leaves had been ripped. No amount of shimmying could hide that. "You want to do something about that, go right ahead. I'd be happy to break in a new partner. Right now, though, I need a new skirt because Rob stepped on it." At least they wore swimsuits under these things. Otherwise, she would have been flashing the audience the whole time. A quarter of them probably wouldn't have minded, but it was a family show: bikinis for Dad, shirtless men for Mom, fire and drums for the kids.

Dave held up his empty hand—the other had a clipboard—in a placating gesture. "Fine, fine, whatever. Just— Whatever." He waved it off and left quickly.

"Rob needs to get fired," Linda said. "He's such an asshole."

Maisie threw her damaged skirt in the bin for that purpose. Someone would try to salvage it later. Fortunately, she had a backup skirt, and pulled it out of her locker. "No argument here."

"He's cute, though." Amy sighed, a dreamy look in her eyes.

Maisie snorted. "You're welcome to him."

"Hey, do you want to go to the beach tomorrow, Maisie?"

Looking over at Linda, Maisie shrugged. "Sure, I guess. Not like I have anything better planned."

"You know he's only asking you out because you keep turning him down." Amy still had that look. It would be annoying if she wasn't nice.

Maisie snorted. "Meaning what? I should just sleep with him and get it over with? No thanks. He is so very much not what I'm looking for. Like I said, he's all yours."

"What's the matter, Maisie?" Bunny's voice held a generous dollop of fake mocking. "Don't you like a guy who's full of himself?" The group of women fell into amused giggles and laughter. They all knew the break would be over before they knew it, though, and set to the task of adjusting costumes and makeup and hair. Chatter turned to plans for tomorrow. Maisie and Linda would hit up one of the tourist beaches and spend the day prowling for beefcake to watch.

Soon enough, they moved out to assemble for the show in the garden setting, around and on an artificial pond. Maisie was the star attraction: the best dancer of the group, and the one Hawaiian girl with icy blue eyes that made her a bird of paradise among the hibiscus. As for the men, none of them stood out among the muscles and six-packs. Rob stepped up beside her, ready to heft her onto his shoulders as soon as the announcer introduced their act.

"Bitch. That was your fault."

"It was not, and you know it, asshole. Watch your damned feet this time or I'll improvise kicking you into the water."

"Whatever."

"Go to hell." She had more to say, but Rob grabbed her and she forced herself to smile. He picked her up and carried her out on his shoulder, both of them playing the part of lovers for the audience. While she shimmied her hips and swung various props to show off her flexibility and skill, the other women danced around her. Three men banged sticks on drums. Another five danced with fire. Rob spotted her on jumps and flips, and lifted her and carried her around.

The last show of the day started in the twilight hours, making the fires flung around by the men more dramatic. Maisie always liked the ones in the dark and near-dark better—it felt magical. When it ended, everyone shucked their costumes and makeup to get out quick. Much to her annoyance, Rob stood by her bicycle where she'd left it locked up for the day, under a freestanding fake tiki torch. She could get a car, but then she'd have to figure out where to park it and pay for the gas. The buses didn't go close enough to her parents' house to be worth it.

"I guess 'beat it, asshole' isn't explicit enough?" The way he stood blocked access to her bike, but only from one side. She stifled a gulp and went around him to unlock the chain.

He scowled with his arms crossed over his chest. "What's your problem?"

Glancing around, she thought she caught sight of a security guard walking past the alley. It made the stabs of apprehension in her gut ease a tiny bit. "My problem? I'm not the one with the problem. Let go of my bike."

Rob spent all day, five days a week, supporting her weight, lifting her, and throwing her around. She had no chance of breaking the grip he had on the top tube of her bike. "Not until you agree to go out with me."

Those words made her blood run cold. She stared at him, knowing she looked scared, and could see in his face that he knew it, too. And he liked it. "Is this seriously the only way you can get a date?" It came out much less scornful and much more breathless than she wanted it to.

Smirking, he grabbed her arm with his other hand, gripping it tightly. "I'll take that as a yes. Let's go."

Stunned by the idea he intended to haul her off whether she wanted to go or not, her mind blanked. He yanked her away from the bike. It took her three stumbling steps to finally form the coherent thought that he wouldn't stop. Something stupid popped into her head as she glanced back, and she said it. "Someone's going to steal my bike, asshole."

He glanced back and dismissed the matter. "I'll buy you a new one."

There had to be a way to get him to let go for a second so she could run for it. Her panicked thoughts chased themselves until the answer stared her in the face. Maisie opened her mouth and screamed. Instead of letting go, he pulled her close and covered her mouth. She bit his finger and jabbed her elbow at his ribs. He still didn't let go. Why didn't he let go? She kicked and squirmed and made as much noise as she could through his hand. Someone would hear it. Someone would stop him, or at least call the cops.

When he reached the car, he thumped her against it, making sure to hit her head. "Shut up," he snarled. "Jesus, just shut up already."

The impact knocked her senseless long enough for him to let go and hit her across the face. Her head snapped to the side with the sharp blow and she crumpled to the ground, curling up to protect herself from more and whimpering. More would come, she knew it, and if she tried to crawl away, it would be worse. After a few seconds of tense waiting, she looked up to see Rob lying limp on the ground, face down, two white men in dark suits standing nearby like sentinels. A third crouched down and checking him over. The fourth stepped close and crouched beside her.

"Are you alright, miss?" They all wore sunglasses, and she saw the little cord going down from his ear and into his collar. He offered her a hand.

For a moment, she stared at it in shock. "More or less?"

"Is he your boyfriend?"

Shaking as she rose to her unsteady feet, she gripped his hand for support. "No." A sharp pinprick on her arm made her look down at it. He'd shoved a syringe full of clear liquid into her upper arm and pushed the plunger down. She blinked, suddenly dizzy.

"Good."

She saw him pull the syringe out and felt numbness seeping across her body. Before she could cry out again, she collapsed into his arms and everything went black.

CHAPTER 1

"Remind me why I thought this was a good idea."

"You never said it was a good idea, you just agreed to do it."

Bobby snorted and shook his head. "Least I know my expectations been met."

Stephen chuckled. "The plan is going swimmingly so far."

"That's for sure." Bobby looked around the holding cell they occupied, not remotely afraid of the four punks they shared it with. A month or so ago, he would've been sitting on the edge of the bench, worried about offending or annoying those guys. Now, they couldn't hurt him even if they all had guns stuffed in their pants. If they tried anyway, the vampire sitting next to him wouldn't let them. "How long you reckon before a suit shows?"

"Man, shut up." One of the punks stood up and cracked his knuckles, radiating menace. His Chicago accent sounded weird to Bobby, even after being around so many different people from so many different places; Bobby's own Southern drawl would always be what sounded 'normal' to him. "Nobody cares about your stupid plan or whatever."

Two of the others egged him on with guttural noises of approval. The fourth guy sat apart and huddled on himself, watching with keen interest.

Bobby and Stephen both turned to look at the guy, neither of them impressed. His black tank top showed off muscles and tattoos, probably from gang affiliation. The guy's baggy jeans had a studded leather belt holding them lower than Bobby liked to wear his, but at least covering most of his dingy white boxers. The guy's hair was slicked back with a black and white pattern bandanna wrapped around his brow.

"Bobby, would it be a problem to add assault to the charges against us?" Stephen addressed him without looking away from the punk.

"So long as you don't kill him," Bobby shrugged, "don't see why."

"I'm not afraid of you," the punk said with a jut of his chin. He took another step forward and held his fists up.

Since Bobby could only see the back of Stephen's head, he had no idea what the punk saw on his face. Whatever it was, the guy paled and gulped. So did the other two. "Your survival instincts are a little dull."

"Oh yeah?" The punk gulped again. He took one step back and low-ered his hands, yet kept the defiant stance. "You talk tough, but I bet you got nothing."

"Wrong answer." Bobby sighed, because it didn't have to be like this. He turned away so he only had to hear the thump and crack as Stephen pursued some small violence. "Don't hurt him bad, neither," he chided. "Cops'll forgive a little scrapping, but they ain't so kind when somebody needs to go to the hospital."

Stephen sat back down beside him, no sign of anything having hap-pened from him. The two other guys, though, had to pick their bold friend up off the floor. "It's not my fault the floor is bare concrete."

"That there is an excuse."

"Excuse, explanation, tomayto, tomahto, whatever."

"If'n this weren't a jail cell, I'd be real disappointed, but they probably got something coming to them."

Stephen laughed again. "I expect we'll see a suit in no more than four hours from when they processed us," he peered up at the clock out of reach beyond the bars, "so anytime now."

Bobby glanced up at the clock, too, wondering what Lily was doing right now. Half past midnight in Chicago meant half past eleven in Colorado. She ought to be asleep. Unless, of course, he decided to be an ass of an idiot who ran off without a word or note to be a stupid hero. At least he was doing something. Jasmine and ten others were still prisoners, and he meant to find them and free them. No matter how stupid this idea might be, it was better than sitting around at the farmhouse, waiting for a clue or something they'd never get.

The door into the area opened, and Stephen smirked. "Right on time."

Bobby turned to see two suits, both looking straight at him and led by the black lady cop that stuck the two of them in here. The one in front paused and said something into his cuff while the other one kept going. "Mitchell and Cant, on your feet, give me your hands. What happened to Ibanez?" No one said anything. Stephen and Bobby dutifully presented their hands and got them slapped with cuffs. "Mmhmm," she said with narrowed eyes.

"It's nice to finally meet you, Mitchell." The suit grabbed Bobby roughly by the arm.

"Am I famous or something? Would you like a signed photograph?"

"I'd like one," Stephen said cheerfully. The other suit grabbed him and hustled him out right behind Bobby.

As they reached the front door of the station, Bobby lifted his hands. "Guys, you know as well as we do the cuffs are kinda silly. If'n we wanted to get gone, we wouldn't be here, don't act like you don't know that. It's insulting."

The suit glanced at his partner, then they nodded to each other. They took the cuffs off and tossed them off to the side without bothering to try to aim for a cop. "What do you want?" Bobby's suit asked as they pushed through the door and into the Chicago night, his hand still firmly gripping Bobby's bicep.

"We're tired of running, of the bickering and stuff."

"Whatever it is about us, it must make the women especially bitchy. It was fine at first. But the girls," Stephen said with a roll of his eyes, "it's like trying to deal with angry cats."

"Seriously not worth it." Bobby nodded his agreement. "You don't stick us with nothing, we come willingly, somebody on your team gets to pitch us a deal for what y'all want from us. We don't like it, we walk away, we leave y'all alone so long as you leave us alone. That's the deal."

The suits stared at them with identical blank expressions. Several long seconds later, one jerked a thumb at the standard issue black SUV illegally parked in front of the station. "We'll have to clear that first. In the meantime, get in the car."

"One of us could just talk to your handlers directly," Stephen offered. "It would save time."

"Fat chance," his suit snorted. "Get in the car."

They got in the car while both suits stayed outside to use their phones. "I ain't sure whether to be insulted or not that they only sent two guys to pick us up." Bobby popped a single dragon off his thumb. It zoomed around the car, looking for anyone hidden in the shadows of the back. It found nothing and returned to him.

"Here's hoping they don't just stick us with something and shoot us in the head."

"D'ya think that would kill you?"

"No idea. Not keen to find out." Stephen sat back casually, adopting the relaxed persona of a Very Important Person waiting to be driven by his chauffeur.

Bobby tapped the buckle of the seatbelt, trying to decide if he wanted to put it on or not. "You reckon they figure it don't matter how many they send?"

"Probably. Why risk four when you can risk just two and get the same result?" Stephen shrugged. "I think they're just goons anyway."

"Should we ask about that old guy?"

"As soon as we mention the name, they'll know we know something and stop treating us like dumb but dangerous kids. We'll become smart dangerous kids, which is kind of a scary thing to old white guys used to being in control."

"Yeah, I guess."

Stephen rolled his shoulders again. "We're here to be agreeable because we're tired of running and tired of bitches telling us what to do. Just remember that and we'll be golden."

Bobby nodded. That was the plan, along with hoping they'd be taken wherever the others could be found and freed, or someplace they could find records to tell them where that might be. As plans went, it lacked subtlety, nuance, and greatness. He'd gotten tired of waiting for a better one.

The suits opened the doors and climbed into the front seats. "Your terms are acceptable." The one in the driver's seat started up the car.

His statement relaxed tension in Bobby's shoulders he hadn't previously been aware of. "Where we going, then? I hope it ain't Salt Lake City."

He ignored Stephen's small cough and elbow nudge.

"No. We'll meet someone in Indianapolis. It's about a three hour drive, give or take."

Bobby let out his own tiny cough, hoping to cover his surprise. How many locations did these guys have? More importantly, these suits didn't need to know how fast the two of them could fly, and didn't need to know how interested both of them were in the location. "Don't suppose we could stop for a bite to eat on the way? I'm starving."

Stephen snorted. "You're always starving."

"I'm a growing boy." Bobby grinned. "I ain't picky, neither. Anything's fine."

"I, on the other hand, am extremely picky."

The suit in the passenger seat turned around with a blank face, the sunglasses keeping the movements of his eyes a mystery. "Define 'picky'."

"I prefer redheads, between ten and five inches shorter than me, clean and sober, in heels."

Passenger Suit's mouth puckered up in annoyed distaste. "We can hit up a drive-through."

"I 'preciate that." Bobby rolled his eyes and shoved Stephen.

"It's the truth," Stephen said, sounding wounded. He looked back at Passenger Suit. "Nothing for me. Get him enough to feed a small army."

Bobby snorted and watched the suit face forward again. With nothing left to do now but sit back and wait, he wound up staring out the window, watching the highway go by. About an hour later, they paused long enough to get some food. His belly full of cheeseburgers and fries, Bobby dozed off for the rest of the trip.

He woke to Stephen jabbing him in the side with an elbow as the SUV rolled through the streets of Indianapolis. The suits kept quiet until they pulled into the well-lit parking lot for a two-story office building. Light peeked through the blinds of three windows on the second floor. They parked next to an identical black SUV.

"This is it," Driver Suit said as he shut off the car.

"Ain't exactly what I was expecting," Bobby said, peering at the building. Nothing about it held any interest, from the blank, whitish walls to the squared shrubs. He thought the place where these guys did their business should have some kind of sinister feel to it. This reminded him of nothing worse than his dentist's office.

"Your expectations aren't really our concern." Passenger Suit hopped out and opened the door for Stephen.

"Do they surgically remove your sense of humor before you're allowed to wear the sunglasses?" Stephen asked.

"Yes," Driver Suit deadpanned as he opened the door on Bobby's side.

Bobby chuckled. "I reckon that actually means no." He chose not to resist when Driver Suit grabbed his arm.

"People keep telling me that no means no, and yes means 'probably'." Stephen let Passenger Suit grip his arm, too.

Feeling a surge of mild paranoia about this too-quiet spot, Bobby let his free arm dangle and popped a dragon off his thumb without comment. If nothing happened, great. If something happened, he'd still have a dragon on the outside.

The suits marched them in through an unlocked door, then up the stairs. On the second floor, Driver Suit knocked on the door for Suite 204, and another suit opened it.

"How many guys in suits y'all got, anyway? Seems like an unlimited supply."

The new suit's mouth went thin, and he slapped Bobby across the face. He tried to, at least. His hand connected with Bobby's face, but he burst into the swarm with the impact, so the suit's hand went right through his head. Hundreds of tiny robot dragons, all outraged that this man dared to hit Bobby, converged on that hand to destroy it.

Surprised, Bobby took a moment to absorb what happened as his mind hovered in the center of the swarm. If he didn't stop them, the dragons would shred the suit's hand and move on to engulf his whole body. They'd kill the suit and this whole trip would be for nothing. Also, a man would be dead, which was a Very Bad Thing, for more reasons than the obvious one.

Stephen shoved the suit to the side while Bobby clamped down on the swarm. "Get a grip," the vampire snarled at the new suit. "We can kill all three of you faster than you can pull out syringes and use them. Remember that."

ASIDE – PAUL

"What do you think?"

Paul watched the minor scuffle through a tinted window, the kind that allowed a person to observe out of sight so long as the light stayed off. One agent gripped his hand in real pain. The two newcomers glared at the agents and moved with the wariness of cobras facing a mongoose. They sat in the chairs suggested by the remaining two agents and seemed to have divided the responsibility for watching the agents by unspoken accord.

He hadn't expected them to look so...normal. The taller one was too pale, but otherwise reminded him of an average college student. Paul could easily picture the guy on his own home campus of Seattle University, and, he noted with a small bite of jealousy, with coeds on both muscled arms. Raymond had that, too.

The other one had about a week's worth of light brown beard to match his shaggy hair, and wore jeans with a blank t-shirt. In the footage he'd seen of the incident at Hill Air Force Base, these two men struck him as monsters. Here, now, they seemed more like earthy movie stars, the kind of men people would meet and comment about how nice and friendly they'd been. Although he didn't appear to qualify as the kind of classically handsome that the girls went ga-ga for, he could imagine this shorter one with a girl-next-door in his arms.

"I can't read anything at all off Cant," he told the other man in the room with him. "He's blank. But he looks like he's not afraid of anything he can see coming, and doesn't have much respect for authority. Mitchell, on the other hand... There's a lot to read from him, too much. It's like he's got—" Struggling under the weight of so much input, he frowned. "Like each individual thread of thought occupies a different part of his mind, and they all crash around together. I think maybe it's the dragons I'm sensing, somehow."

"You think each dragon has some part of his mind?"

"I don't know." Paul shook his head. "Maybe if I could read just one dragon, separate from all the others, I could answer the question."

"So your talent is useless with these two."

"I guess so." Disappointed with this truth, Paul sighed. He wanted to help. "Maybe if I was in the room with them—"

"No." The other man pulled his sunglasses out of the breast pocket of his suit jacket. "They don't know any of you are working with us yet. I'd like to keep it that way for as long as possible."

Paul nodded and put his hand on the glass. This close, his icy blue, almond shaped eyes were reflected back at him, but he was more interested in the two men on the other side of the glass. "Are we really related?"

"Blood tests have confirmed you all share one parent, yes."

"How did they wind up being such cold killers, then?" It bothered him, a lot, that he had half siblings who could murder people.

"Everyone reacts to power differently."

Nodding, Paul sighed. He knew that. He studied psychology, it just seemed more disturbing when it hit so close to home, so to speak. "What are you going to do?"

"Offer them a job."

"What?"

"What kind of prison could hold them? It would be better to have them on our team, with some kind of control on them, than to try to find some way to stuff them in a box. They've already proven they're willing to kill to get free, and capable of a fair amount of mayhem. Besides, if we can flip them, they know where we can find the rest." He covered his ordinary hazel eyes with the sunglasses. "Put your earbud in. I want your opinions as I talk to them."

Paul nodded again and pulled the small device out of his pocket, then stuck it in his ear. "Is this thing working?"

"Yes. Since you can't get anything from their minds, just pay attention to body language and tell me if you feel strongly they're lying or obfuscating."

"Right. Got it." Paul watched while he opened the door and walked into the other room, hoping he'd be able to read these guys well enough. Lives might depend on it, maybe even his own.

CHAPTER 2

"Gentlemen." That voice sounded oddly familiar, and Bobby turned to see who walked in through the side door. The sunglasses did a lot to make him just another anonymous suit, but that chin tugged on his memory. He'd seen this one before and recognized him. Realizing his identity took him about the same amount of time as it took the guy to pace in and sit down behind the desk, looking like he owned it.

At the time, he'd been FBI Special Agent Steve Privek. Had he actually been an FBI agent then? Bobby reached up without thinking and rubbed his jaw where the man had socked him a good one about six weeks ago. "You're kinda far from Atlanta."

Privek smirked. "So are you, Mitchell."

"You're the one what made me leave in the first place."

"The situation was, perhaps, mishandled in some ways."

Bobby glared at Privek. Are you joking? You framed me for a murder and chained me up like a dog."

"I'm sure that's how you see it." Privek laced his hands together on the desk and leaned forward. "I'm prepared to offer you a deal. Are you here to listen or to address past grievances?"

Stephen reached over and put a restraining hand on Bobby's arm. "We're listening."

This wasn't the time to blow up at Privek and Bobby knew it. The dragons hated this situation and it made him crankier than he ought to be. The contact with Stephen reminded him why he sat in this office, and he snapped his mouth shut, leaning back in the chair with a glower. He could listen, but he didn't have to be happy about it.

"Good. What I have to offer you is a chance to work for the betterment of your country by applying your unique abilities to problems we find difficult to solve with current manpower and technology."

"Is that what you were gonna offer when—" Stephen's hand squeezed his arm painfully, making Bobby stop. A little harder and it would have become dragons.

"What he means is that we're concerned about petty things like bodily autonomy and right of refusal for requests we find objectionable."

One of Privek's eyebrows arched up over the sunglasses. "You'll have to prove we can trust you. After what happened in Salt Lake, we're a little hesitant to just give you whatever you want."

"Being shot kinda makes a guy get surly."

"You wouldn't have been shot if you hadn't already killed three of our men."

"Which was only 'cause—"

Stephen cut him off again. "Bobby. You're not helping."

Nodding, Bobby shut his mouth again. He had to remember that he'd come here for Jasmine, not for himself. Every time he opened his mouth here, he put himself before her, and she didn't deserve that. Worse, he put himself before all of them. While they had a few he didn't much mind doing that to, most of them ought to get better from him.

"I won't speak for Bobby, but I'm definitely interested. What could I expect for the first twenty-four hours?"

"We'll want to run you through a full physical and take some samples for testing."

"What kind of testing?" Stephen frowned. "I'm not interested in being anyone's lab rat."

Privek nodded his understanding. "Just drawing some blood and taking a swab of DNA for examination. After that, we'll want a full explanation of everything you know about that makes you different from a normal person, then we'll assign you missions based upon your abilities. From what we already know of what you can each do, you'd both be well suited to war zone duties."

"I ain't no soldier." Bobby shifted in his seat, annoyed that the idea of actually doing soldiery things made him wonder if Lily would be more attracted to him for it.

"I understand that," Privek said curtly, "but what you can do would be useful to other soldiers. This is about saving lives, gentlemen. A small army of people with your type of capabilities could end most wars with very little loss of life, on both sides."

Bobby sat and glared at the desk. Stephen, though, leaned in and seemed very interested. "I'm not sure how useful I can be in a desert environment, but I'm willing to do what I can to help soldiers come home. Can this be provisional, with the sample-taking after the first mission? I'm hesitant to just give that up right now. It feels violating on some level. I want to know I'm on the right side of the line before I go all in."

Privek pursed his lips and furrowed his brow. After a long pause, he finally said, "Very well. We don't need anything from Mitchell anyway. Hagen will take you to your next destination, where you'll be looked over and questioned about your capabilities."

"If it ain't too much trouble, we'd rather work together than apart."

"I'll make a note." Privek stood up and gave them each a nod without offering his hand to shake. "I hope this is the start of a long partnership, and that we can put all the messy business from before behind us."

Stephen stood with an echoing nod. "So do I."

Bobby stood and grunted his unenthusiastic assent, not caring if that bothered Privek or not. He watched the agent leave the room and turned his mild glower on Stephen. They probably had some kind of setup to listen to whatever they might say in here, so he kept his mouth shut. The vampire wordlessly headed for the other door, the one they used before. Having nothing better to do, Bobby followed. Passenger Suit stood waiting for them alone, checking his phone. At least they didn't get stuck with Touchy Suit.

"I'm Hagen," Passenger Suit said as he looked up. "We'll be heading east. If either of you need to use the bathroom, this is a good time."

"I don't have such petty mortal concerns." Stephen smirked, his humor slipping back on.

Bobby rolled his eyes and headed for the door Hagen pointed out. He needed to settle down. They took a job working for Privek. The dragons seethed inside about it. Heckbiscuits, he seethed inside about it. If he found out Privek had only been an FBI agent following orders before, he might decide to be more charitable about the whole thing. Until then, he wanted to do things to the man that would horrify Momma.

Speaking of Momma, why didn't he think to ask that surveillance be taken off of her house? They might do it anyway, given they had him here now. He still should have asked. Maybe he should teach people how to be as lousy at negotiation as him. Hannah would've handled all this much better. Lizzie could probably have gotten more, too. On second thought, her idea would be to blow stuff up until she got what she wanted, which might not really qualify as 'better'.

At least this mission thing should help people, even if it meant knowing Privek officially pulled his strings. How did that saying go? Good done in the name of Evil is still Good. He splashed some water on his face and stared at himself in the mirror. "You sure you wanna do this?" Thankfully, his reflection didn't answer. The question did galvanize the dragons, though, reminding them why he'd just given up his autonomy to Privek. They had to do something. This qualified as 'something'.

He toweled his face off and took a deep breath. "Just don't forget this is all for them," he told his reflection. "Just don't forget about them, no matter what."

CHAPTER 3

Ten hours later, Bobby and Stephen sat on a couch in the living room of a big old house. Hagen had disappeared to get some sleep after the long drive, and they now faced a man in a normal suit and holding a clipboard. He'd diligently scribbled down their names and now waited patiently for them to explain their superpowers.

Instead of using words, Bobby popped one dragon off his hand. Its fingertip disappeared, the end of the knuckle smooth as if it had originally grown that way. The dragon swooped around the room, chirping its annoyance at this whole process. "My whole body's made of 'em," he told the guy. "Hundreds, maybe over a thousand." It landed on Stephen's shoulder and quieted.

"They eat gears and stuff. I still need to eat, too. One gets smashed or shot or blown up or whatever, the others eat it and I get a sore spot for a bit. They do what I tell 'em to, but can do simple stuff themselves. If'n they get mighty angry, they can blow fire, but I ain't sure they can just do that whenever. Not real good at killing, but the swarm can take a guy down if'n we gotta."

The guy nodded and wrote on his clipboard. Bobby suspected they had cameras recording this interview, too. "Are the dragons 'they' or 'we'?"

Bobby shrugged. "Yes."

He looked up gave Bobby a hard, frowning stare. "What's that sup-posed to mean?"

"Dunno. If'n I figure a way to tell you, I will." Bobby shrugged again.

Stephen snickered. "I, on the other hand, am easier to explain."

After smoothing his expression and flipping a page over the top of the clipboard, the guy said, "Go ahead."

"I'm a fairly classical vampire, though I have no issues with garlic or holy symbols. I'm very sensitive to sunlight and burn easily, more than a person with fair skin. I couldn't say if I catch fire under prolonged expo-sure, and am not interested in learning the truth of that. Other than that, I have the superhuman strength, can fly, regenerate, and drink blood. I have no capability to handle food or other liquids and no longer have need of a bathroom. What happens to the blood in my digestive tract is a mystery I cannot explain, and again, I'm not especially interested in solving it."

The suit nodded and scribbled. "Does sunblock work?"

"Briefly. I tried SPF 70 once on the back of my hand, it started to redden in five minutes instead of five seconds. Clothing works just fine, anything that ordinarily protects from sunburn."

"Ya know, technically, you do have a problem with garlic," Bobby pointed out.

Stephen smirked. "Yes, well, it's not really confined to garlic. All food is problematic. It doesn't repel me is the point, nothing does."

The suit didn't find that funny. "From what I saw you're both per-fectly fine with killing?"

"No, not really." Bobby shook his head.

Stephen pursed his lips and looked off at the wall. "It's not some-thing I prefer to do. Drinking blood is fairly primal, though. The instincts are there, and can be difficult to suppress."

Bobby squirmed. "I only did take down three of your guys. Them first two, the dragons were kinda..." He shifted again. "I lost control of the swarm, they went berserk on account of what was done to me up to then. That third one, he tried to shoot me and a kid, and it didn't look like he was gonna stop. I don't got a whole lotta control over that —once they're looking to kill, they're looking to kill."

The guy huffed and wrote something else down. With one brow arched, he glanced from Bobby to Stephen and back. "If you were asked to kill someone, like an assassination, would you be able or willing to do that?"

Bobby looked at Stephen, who shrugged. He scratched at his beard and frowned. "I guess if'n it was a bad guy who done things what ain't right, then maybe, yeah. Call it a case-by-case sorta thing, but it ain't neither of us's first choice. I'm good at scouting, and getting in and outta places."

"My talents seem obvious to me," Stephen said, "but put bluntly, I am good at being very difficult to kill, and incapacitating those who block my passage."

The suit nodded. "Alright, this is good enough for now. I'm pretty sure they'll want to send you to a war zone to try to put a dent in the insurgency, but we'll see." He stood to leave the room. "Can I get you anything while you wait? It might be a few hours."

"I am kinda hungry," Bobby nodded. "Whatever's lying around is fine."

Stephen rolled his neck to the side, cracking it. "If you have any females willing to take one for the team, I could use a few pints."

"I'll..." The guy frowned again and tucked the clipboard under one arm. "I'll see what I can do." He walked out, leaving them sitting in silence.

On the way here Bobby saw the road signs, so he knew they'd come to Virginia. This wasn't the same place he woke up in that lab a month ago. He knew nothing else about it so far. It seemed unlikely this house played a major role in Privek's operation. He'd be stupid to send them to a location with strategic value.

"Basement," Stephen said after the door clicked shut.

"Yeah, that's my guess, too. Otherwise, they'd have more security for the ground floor."

Stephen stood and stretched. They'd both slept on the drive here, and hadn't had a chance to walk around much since arriving in mid-morning. "I wonder how long they'll keep us waiting."

Tired of sitting, Bobby followed suit and paced to the window. He pushed the gauzy white curtain aside and peered out. Hagen's black SUV sat parked outside, no other vehicles in sight. "I wonder where they put the rest of the cars. Round the back, maybe, so it don't look like there's folks here so much."

"Makes sense to me. I suppose they'd get a little annoyed if we went snooping around."

"Probably." Bobby shrugged. "Reckon they're gonna ask us to take out terrorists?"

"Yes. I also expect they'll use a very broad, overly inclusive definition of the word 'terrorist'."

Sighing heavily, Bobby kept looking out the window. He'd seen the trees screening the house from the highway on the way in and watched the leaves sway in a breeze. "Yeah, I reckon."

"More interesting to me is what they'll do about my nutritional needs."

"You just ate last night. I thought you could go a coupla days between."

"I can," Stephen nodded, "but I don't like to. It's best if I get at least a few pints every twelve hours, or a good, heavy meal once a day. That blonde was too skinny to take much from her. Before that, my last real feed was two days before that. It's getting a little dark in here." Without any further explanation, Bobby knew Stephen referred to his Hunger taking over, bit by bit.

"Maybe you oughta been a little more upfront about that."

"Group like this probably has a bunch of people who'll do anything to keep their jobs. The suits strike me as zealots."

They both heard footsteps coming their way and went quiet. When the door opened, a brunette with dusky olive skin and brown eyes walked in. She wore a forest green suit with black pumps. Her eyes immediately went to Stephen's, then Bobby's, a flicker of recognition lighting them up. "Hablas español o parlez-vous français?"

She had a smooth voice, one that rolled around in Bobby's head and made him want to like her. If he had to guess, he'd say she was Spanish or Mexican, because he understood the first two words well enough, and recognized the accent. "No, ma'am, sorry."

Stephen also shook his head, and offered her his hand. "This both complicates and simplifies things," he muttered with a smirk. "Stephen," he said, gesturing to himself.

"Elena. English little. You..." She trailed off with a frown.

Raising a hand solemnly, Stephen gave her a small, gallant bow. "No harm to you, I promise. Sit?" He pointed to the couch.

Though he didn't really want to watch, Bobby had only seen Stephen feed once. At the time, other things had been going on and he hadn't been all there. Curiosity made him half-watch from the side while still standing at the window.

Elena perched on the edge of the couch, facing him and watching Stephen. She glanced at Bobby and back to Stephen. Bobby thought he'd be nervous in her position, too. Her boss sent her into a room with two unknown men she had no real way to communicate with, probably without telling her exactly what to expect.

"Relax," Stephen said softly, slipping onto the couch beside her. "Five minutes." Holding up his hand with all five fingers out, he used it to distract her while he seized her arm and licked her wrist. Elena's eyes went wide and she gasped. Stephen brushed her thick hair away from her neck and plunged his fangs in.

Elena moaned and grabbed Stephen's jeans. The small sounds of arousal sounded like "Liam" a few times. Her body pushed back against him. Suddenly, Bobby felt like a voyeur, watching his buddy have sex with a random girl, and he turned away from it.

Worse, the scene reminded him of kissing Lily a few days ago. Not only did he regret not leaving her a note, he couldn't wipe away the memory. He'd managed to get a few minutes alone with her in the woods around the farm. The second he touched the small of her back under her shirt, she used the pet name for her dead husband. Everything got awkward in a hurry.

"Much better." Distracted from his thoughts, Bobby saw Stephen licking his lips, Elena draped across him. His eyes snapped open and he slipped out from behind her. When he'd settled her on the couch, he adjusted his jeans. "That'll keep me for a day or two."

"She alright?"

"She'll be fine." He reached down and checked her pulse with two fingers. "Mmm, I maybe took a little more than I ought to have."

"She ain't dead, I hope."

"No, just weak. She won't be down for long, though. Probably." Stephen shrugged. "All I know for sure is Kris bounces right back with just a night of sleep."

Bobby snorted. Stephen's new girlfriend may or may not be real, but the vampire definitely had a steady source of blood keeping him away from the farmhouse. "What'd you tell her, anyway?"

"I said I needed to do a thing for my brother and couldn't say how long I'd be gone. If I get a chance, I'll call her." He waved the subject off. "I suppose we ought to let them know she's out cold." He paced over to the door and peered out. Someone must have been standing right there, because Bobby heard Stephen say, "I'm done. She probably needs the rest of the day off."

The way he said it made Bobby feel dirtier than he had a moment before, like he'd helped Stephen rape the woman. He looked back out the window and shook it off. The guy needed to eat to live and not be a depraved monster, after all. Behind him, someone walked in and carried Elena out without a word.

Outside, he saw a dark blue sedan pull in and park. A man in a brown military uniform stepped out of the driver's door, then opened the rear door for what Bobby assumed must be a military officer of some kind. Since he knew what Marines looked like, he knew this man wasn't one. Navy wore white, he thought, and he knew Air Force used blue, so the tan uniform had to mean an Army guy. Given Lizzie blew up half of that base in Utah, he decided to be glad they hadn't brought an Air Force guy.

"I'm thinking they want us to work for the Army."

Stephen paced over and peered out over Bobby's head. "Apparently.

I guess this means we get to kill terrorists and find land mines."

"I ain't sure how I feel about that."

Dropping himself back on the couch, Stephen shrugged. "If they're going to send soldiers to do this stuff anyway, we might as well do it and keep those guys from getting shot or blown up. Maybe we can even put the fear of Allah into them enough to make them tell us stuff."

"I don't speak no Arab."

The door opened and the Army officer they saw outside walked in with his hat under his arm and a brown folder in his hand. His name tag read 'Delane'. Bobby had no idea what all the colored bits and rank bobs meant, other than this guy had more of them than his Daddy had. Hagen escorted him in. As they walked in, Delane nodded to something Hagen must have said moment before.

"Boys." Delane had the kind of stern voice that commanded attention and demanded obedience. "I'm Lieutenant Colonel Delane, US Army. I understand you have some unusual talents and would like to use them to serve your country as quietly as possible."

Every time he thought he understood what was going on with the suits, something came up that destroyed Bobby's notions. He didn't understand how guys who pretended to be FBI, CIA, and who knows what else would have a genuine Army officer guy here to recruit them. Were these guys actually part of some legitimate government agency that somehow, nobody actually knew about? "Yeah, that's a fair way to put it."

"Mitchell, right?" Bobby nodded and Delane opened his folder to read from it. "I understand your father was an excellent Marine."

"Didn't stop him from getting killed." If they wanted to bring his Daddy into this, he had no reason not to tell it like he saw it.

Delane barely reacted, giving Bobby only a tiny jut of his chin in response. The man probably dealt with unhappy families all the time. He turned his attention to Stephen. "Allen Cant was a good soldier, too."

"Happily," Stephen sneered, "my older brother is still alive and no longer in harm's way." It might be a challenge for both of them to avoid mentioning Matthew and his PTSD issues. They had to, for everyone's sake.

"If you two are willing, maybe we can do something to keep more of our military men and women alive and unharmed."

"Sounds like a plan," Bobby said hurriedly, wanting to avoid a discussion that would reveal more than they wanted to. "We ain't real keen to be doing assassinations, though."

"I told him that," Hagen said.

"And I understand. It takes a certain kind of person to handle that kind of mission, and there's no shame in not being one." Delane took the chair and gestured for Bobby to sit on the couch beside Stephen. "It seems to me you'd be best used as a team, accomplishing objectives we'd ordinarily send a larger group to handle. Assaulting strongholds, retrieving prisoners, clearing the way for demolitions and other experts, that sort of thing."

"We agreed to take on one mission and evaluate whether we want to work for you after that."

Delane nodded. "That's fine. We'll need you to run through some basic training, so you're familiar with how things work, and some routine survival training. It won't take long, considering your unusual abilities. We'll get you some uniforms, too, and all in all, you can be out in the field in three or four days, depending on when we can schedule the flight to get you out there. We'll give you a few objectives, and when those are complete, if you're not willing to continue out there, that'll be that."

The only thing Bobby didn't like about this plan had to do with remaining out of communication with the farm. They knew that might be a problem when they left, and decided to chance it. He should have left a note. Matthew knew. He wanted to come along. They'd turned him down for two reasons: he had no control over his shapeshifting and he couldn't fly.

It had taken the pair of them about nine hours to fly to Chicago. Driving would've taken at least fifteen, and they would've needed to take someone else's car. Bobby wished they could've brought him along, if only so he didn't have to face the rest of the group when they discovered Bobby and Stephen missing. The memory of Matthew ripping arms off at Hill made him certain they'd chosen wisely on that front.

He could hardly wait to find out how they all reacted to the two of them taking matters into their own hands. It probably depended a lot on how successful they were and how long it took to get that success. As long as Lily stopped short of hating him for this, he could probably live with it. "Might as well get started, then." Bobby hopped to his feet and did his best to seem eager to be on his way to glory for God and country.

Less eager, Stephen stood and offered Delane his hand to shake. "Yes, I think we're your men."

Taking the hand and shaking it, Delane stood, too, and then shook hands with Bobby. "Just so we're clear, it's my understanding this will all be done in a classified fashion. That is, only those who absolutely must know who you are and what you're doing will."

CHAPTER 4

"These are my clothes." Bobby said it again, for the hundredth time, as he and Stephen walked off the plane depositing them at some base in Afghanistan. They'd been shoved onto a flight to Germany, then another one to someplace in Turkey, and now here, to the country where both Lily's husband and Bobby's father were killed. Would either she or Momma be proud of him for doing this? Doubtful. His Daddy would be, though.

Stephen huddled in on himself, shrinking down in the harsh light. Though they both wore hats and sunglasses and combat boots and full Army desert camouflage BDUs, the sunshine beat down and reflected off everything. The vampire also wore gloves and a balaclava. With every square inch of flesh covered, he had to look like he ought to be sweating his skin off. As for Bobby, the heat didn't bother him much. The dryness of the air, on the other hand, took his breath away and instantly made him thirsty.

It took them twenty minutes and a Corporal to find the guy they'd been instructed to report to. He couldn't be military, because he wore a suit with no jacket. Everyone around him dressed the same, in business attire with jackets slung across the backs of chairs. It seemed likely these folks were civilians in Intelligence, which made their being directed to him make sense. Sort of.

"Mitchell, Cant, I'm Klein." Shaking hands with them, Klein brought them to a table with an unattended laptop sitting open. He had that average white guy look to him. If Bobby saw this guy walking down the street, he'd just assume he was an upstanding citizen with a professional job, then not think anything else about him at all.

"I've been told you're a two man team of specialists capable of doing things I'm not allowed to ask about, and can handle objectives that ordinarily take a squad or two." Klein looked to both of them for confirmation. They both nodded. "Okay. I've got a couple of missions that you might be able to handle." He tapped on the laptop, bringing up photographs. "Three different ones, see if any of them sound doable to you.

"One: a town too far north for us to do anything but airstrikes that we suspect is a weapons stockpile but can't prove it without sending in a ground unit. Two: a warlord working against us holed up in a secure compound surrounded by civilians. Three: a cave system that needs to be explored. We think it's mined and there might be an easy ambush against us in it."

"Yeah, we can probably handle those," Bobby nodded, fiddling with his sunglasses.

"Shouldn't be a problem. We'll need maps and..." Stephen had his sunglasses off, too, and he scanned the room. Pointing to a brunette that happened to be the most attractive woman in the room, the corners of his mouth curled up. "Can you spare her for the rest of the day?"

"What? Wait, back up." Klein furrowed his brow. "Which mission?"

"They ain't too far apart, looks like," Bobby said with a shrug. "All three."

"Uh, okay." Klein followed the line of Stephen's gaze. "Then what do you need Jenny for? She's a secretary."

Though he didn't want to, Bobby shoved aside his squeamishness. "Pretty sure you just said you weren't s'posed to ask questions."

By this point, Jenny had noticed the interest in her and joined the three men. "Did you need something, Pete?" She had a pretty, open face, and Bobby knew he'd be interested in her if he hadn't met Lily.

"I'm in need of assistance, Jenny, please, this way." Stephen sounded so gallant and gentlemanly. She glanced at Klein, who sighed and nodded. The pair of them disappeared out of the tent.

"He ain't gonna rape her or nothing." At least, Bobby hoped he wouldn't. The vampire's morality on the subject had been left somewhat vague, and Bobby had no idea how devoted he'd really become to Kris in the few weeks he'd allegedly known her.

Klein's frown deepened, and he sighed again. "She's my responsibility."

"She ain't being hurt. You got my word. He's just got a peculiar...uh..." Giving up, Bobby shrugged. Gimme all what we need to know, 'specially about this warlord guy and what he done to deserve killing, and we'll leave soon as he's— Soon."

Ten minutes later, Bobby had three maps with dots on them and understood the three missions well enough to get them done. When Stephen joined him, coming from the medical tent, he said, "Klein's a mite worried about Jenny."

"She'll be fine. I was careful not to knock her out. They," he jerked a thumb over his shoulder, "think she's dehydrated, which is more or less accurate."

Deciding to take what Stephen said at face value, Bobby handed a few things over. "I got maps and a headset for ya. They'll have someone who can interpret standing by starting two hours from now. I just wanna stop and grab some food and water, and then we can get going, 'less you want to wait for nightfall. Looks like it'll take us about two hours to get to the weapon place, the other two are in that same region, maybe a half hour to the caves, another fifteen to twenty to the warlord."

"What time is it here?"

Checking his nice new watch, courtesy of Hagen, Bobby said, "It's just past three in the afternoon. Klein said it'll get dark a little after six."

Stephen looked around, though Bobby could only tell because he actually turned his head. "Get what you need then let's get going. I'm covered up, we might as well travel. We can wait there just as easily as here."

Bobby nodded and clapped him on the arm. "Meet me on the north end. I'll be quick as I can." Without waiting for a response, he jogged off to find supplies. With the First Lieutenant rank insignias they'd been loaned, he had no trouble requisitioning as much food and water as he could stuff into his pockets and a small pack.

Twenty minutes later, he found Stephen on the north end of the base, looking over the maps in the shade of a tent structure. Bobby passed the pack over because he wouldn't be able to carry it himself, and they took to the air. They went up high and fast enough to not be a spectacle for people on the ground, then headed to the first site.

For the next two hours, Bobby had nothing to do but fly and think. The dragons hated it when he thought a lot. With no distractions, it happened anyway. Everything came back to Lily. She called him 'Bas' out of habit. She'd never kissed anyone but her late husband. Knowing that didn't lessen the sting.

He genuinely liked her, and told her so, and she seemed to feel the same. Then she slipped and made it clear she considered him a stand-in for a dead man, allowed into her arms as a replacement. Sure, he'd more or less stepped into the Dad role for her son, but that didn't mean he wanted to be Sebastian Thatcher, Sr., Part Two. He wanted to be a whole new movie.

Dammit, he had to go up against a dead man. It would never be a fair fight. Sebastian got to be safely tucked away in her memories, more perfect than he'd really been because of nostalgia. Bobby, on the other hand, screwed up and said stupid new crap every day. And now this.

He'd have to beg for her forgiveness. Often, probably. Why were they even out here, doing this? Was this what the suits were having the eleven they grabbed doing? Why did they torture him if they wanted super-soldiers? Maybe they were stupid and thought...something stupid.

Thinking back, which he'd done umpteen times since he and Jayce and Alice and Ai broke out of that lab, he figured none of those science guys figured any of them might wake up on their own. Someone said he had high metabolism, which meant he woke up, and when he freaked out, he got the others off their drugs, too. They escaped...

What if he figured wrong? Those guys could've constructed the circumstances he woke up under. He imagined how it might have turned out if he woke up with someone 'rescuing' him from that. Until given a reason not to, he would've trusted that person implicitly.

Privek said 'mistakes were made'. Bobby had assumed he meant the framing, the arrest, and that part. What if the 'mistake' had been more about not having everything ready when he woke up? They probably learned from that mistake. His thoughts turned to Jasmine and how that could be applied to her.

As much as he liked her, Jasmine wasn't the brightest bulb in the box. A scenario took shape, where she woke up and found suits telling her things she believed, then showing her the footage from Hill. She'd nod along and agree that kind of destruction needed to be prevented in the future. They'd find a way to use Will's unknown whereabouts to motivate her.

Before he managed to follow these ideas to more concrete suspicions and conclusions, Stephen angled downward. With the sun setting, they chose a spot in the craggy hills outside the small town they planned to assault first. The cluster of buildings surrounded on three sides by barren, rocky inclines would be rough to reach on foot or by vehicle. The fourth side must be what they used to actually come and go—it was open ground and the approach could be seen for miles.

"We'll wait for true darkness, then drop in from above."

Bobby re-formed and pulled out an MRE, leaning back against a rock. "Stephen, I'm starting to wonder if we're actually working for the bad guys."

Stephen kept his eyes on the village. He didn't answer immediately. Bobby waited in silence, figuring he'd been thinking about other things for the past two hours. "I have a feeling that we'll discover this isn't about black and white so much as it is about methods and ideology. We've attacked and killed for our freedom. They've attacked and tried to kill for what seems to be a desire for control over us. It's a pretty classic type of conflict, really—it happens over and over again throughout history. My guess is they generally see us as weapons, and the more we act like that, the more likely they are to assert we aren't human, aren't citizens, aren't deserving of basic rights."

If he wasn't sure of it before, Bobby now knew without a doubt that Stephen had more brains than him. "I got the feeling when Privek said they made mistakes, he meant something different from what it sounded like."

Stephen nodded. "That's probably true. Some part of me wonders why they kept that list in that file cabinet. From what you described, it seemed like a serendipitous event, Ai finding it, but I just have to wonder if it was left there for a reason. Maybe you were supposed to find it. Maybe every file cabinet had several copies of that list distributed through the folders. Your escape could have been part of someone's larger plan. To what end, I don't know, but it's a thing to consider."

His mouth being full gave Bobby the chance to temper his initial reaction without saying something dumb. "I ain't sure I'm up for tinfoil hat theories yet."

Stephen grinned. "Yes, it does seem a little overly Machiavellian, doesn't it?"

"I never heard that word before, but if it means complicated and creepy, sure." Taking the canteen from where Stephen set it for him, he downed a few swallows of water to wash the food down. His garbage went back into the pocket he pulled the thing from in the first place. "I'm good, and it's pretty close to dark."

Still grinning, Stephen pointed vaguely towards the village. "How do you want to do this?"

"Well," Bobby shrugged, "I figure I can dragon through and see what there is to see. If'n we find anything, I tell you and we go blow it all up."

"Seems reasonable to me. I'll see if I can come up with anything more detailed for the 'blow it all up' part. Given that neither of us is really exceptional at that sort of mayhem."

"Yeah, we're kinda more people mayhem than stuff mayhem."

"Agreed. A shame we couldn't bring Matthew. But, c'est la vie. I'll come hang out over the village and wait for you there."

"La vee." Bobby blew into the swarm and flew with Stephen to the village. The vampire stayed a few hundred yards up while the dragons dove into the buildings, flying through in whatever way seemed least likely to get them noticed. He couldn't micromanage them all, so he had to rely on them understanding his demand to avoid being seen.

This was the first time he'd ever dispersed the swarm so much that no central glob of dragons remained. To his surprise, his 'mind' didn't automatically hitch a ride with any particular one or grouping so much as float in the center of them all.

Pushing that oddity aside, Bobby watched through their eyes, able to handle getting all of it at once. They dove in through windows and zoomed under doors, all on the lookout for any of the things Bobby considered 'a pile of weapons'. Room after room of house after house, they kept going and going, sometimes stopping to peer at things. Half an hour later, the swarm came together around Stephen and urged him back to where they initially landed. He reformed and immediately shrugged.

"'Less they got a different definition of 'weapon' than I do, there ain't nothing here. I mean, every house's got at least one military looking gun, but ain't none of 'em with more'n two or three. That don't seem like a 'stockpile' to me."

"You sure there aren't any caves or tunnels where they might be stashed?"

"If'n they got anything like that, it's hid pretty good. Didn't see nothing weird, neither. These folks don't even got 'lectricity and running water, let alone stuff to make chemicals and stuff."

Putting his hand up to his earpiece, Stephen said, "Cant and Mitchell reporting in at the suspected weapons depot." He paused for a moment and rolled his eyes. "If you wanted to have some sort of code, you should have set it up before we left. ...These people have personal arms, but no stockpiles or armory. They've actually got goats they're actually herding.

"...That seems a bit extreme. What they do have wouldn't even raise an eyebrow in Texas. In fact, some of them might be accused of being pussies for having so few firearms." Stephen's face slowly went annoyed, until he looked more or less like he'd swallowed a lemon. "I believe I have a duty under the Geneva Convention to tell you to go fuck yourself, Klein. Unless you can give me some actual reason why we should attack an obviously non-military target posing no apparent threat, you can farm that job out to someone else. We don't murder civilians for no reason."

Bobby glanced back towards the village, able to guess what Klein wanted them to do. "I could take another look, to make sure. Or we could let them capture us." The idea of allowing himself be taken prisoner to work the place from the inside while he was in the middle of doing the same thing with the suits gave him a humorless smirk.

Stephen sighed. "We'll go back in and take another look around to see if we missed anything. I'll contact you when we've finished that." He pulled the earpiece out and stuck it in his pocket. "Did either of us say something to suggest we were interested in spree killings?"

"Nope. You wanna just stay here?"

"Nah, let's go see if there's a welcome wagon for visitors new to town."

"Here's hoping they got somebody what speaks English."

He was already halfway into the swarm as Stephen said, "Anything is possible." They flew together to the nearest edge of the village, where Bobby reformed next to Stephen as he landed. From there, they walked among the buildings, looking around like anyone in a new place would. From his earlier foray, Bobby knew the layout and guided Stephen to the center. There, a ring of rocks marked the edge of a round hole in the ground filled with water.

A woman in a blue dress with a black headscarf, carrying a jug likely intended to hold water, stopped at the edge of the small empty space around the well and took in a surprised breath. She said something that sounded alarmed and confused.

"Ma'am, any chance you speak English?" Bobby figured he might as well try. He pronounced the words slowly and carefully.

Instead of answering, she shouted, her intent clear enough: calling for help. Within seconds, doors all around slammed open and out came men with those assault rifles Bobby saw earlier. Both he and Stephen put their hands up, but that didn't stop some of them interposing themselves between the two men and the woman. She scurried off. The men stayed.

"Good evening," Stephen said, sounding friendly and polite. "Do any of you speak English?"

"I do, some." One man nodded to call attention to himself. He had a thick accent. "What you want, Americans?"

Bobby looked at Stephen, who returned it, they both shrugged, and Stephen indicated him with a jerk of his chin. Bobby sighed—elected spokesperson again. "We're lost. Our boss thinks there's a bunch of weapons lying around somewhere near here, but we can't find 'em."

Stephen almost managed to stifle down a chuckle. "We have no intention of harming anyone here, so long as you don't shoot first."

The man stared at them skeptically. "You come to poison well, to murder women and children?"

"No, sir. Ain't got no reason to hurt folk what're just doing what you can to survive out here. Must be tough, on account you all got weapons like that in easy reach. Folks come out here all the time just to harass y'all?"

"You are here."

Man had a point. Bobby grinned. "Ain't that the truth. We ain't here to cause no trouble, though."

"This is silly." Stephen put his hands down. "Are you aware of any reason why anyone might want to destroy your village? Because we were sent here to look for weapons you obviously don't have, and when we reported back that fact, we were ordered to kill you all anyway, something we don't particularly want to do."

The man took a few seconds to think about that, then he spoke rapidly with the other men. Bobby followed Stephen's example and put his hands down while the locals chatted. After a few minutes, during which Bobby wondered if they'd made a mistake, the lead man said, "Come, we show."

Bobby and Stephen shared a surprised look, then both shrugged and followed the man. Only three of the men escorted them, plus their interpreter, and all kept guns handy. They went to the edge of the village, the same one they arrived through. "Taliban come here," the man explained as they walked. "We give them one girl and metal, or they kill two men. Americans come to war, Taliban want more, but we have no more girls to give. They take goats, food, cloth, and metal. Americans give us weapons for metal, we fight back. Taliban not come anymore."

He pulled up what was apparently a fake shrub anchored by some kind of plaster brick and scraped dirt away from a wooden trap door. It had an iron ring he grabbed and yanked on to open the door. "You go down, look, see."

Not expecting anything like this, Bobby blinked a few times, then realized he was supposed to be delving down into that hole. He pulled out his little flashlight and clicked it on, then crouched down beside the hole and shone the beam around in there. "I reckon somebody done mixed some papers up or something." It had no ladder or stairs. They'd have no problems getting in and out. "That sounds kinda familiar."

He jumped down and stumbled at the bottom. Looking up, he guessed the ceiling had to be about ten feet high. "It's fair sized, come on down," he called up for Stephen.

"Thank you for showing us this," he heard Stephen say, then the vampire also jumped in, making it look like gravity actually affected him.

"Ain't this a surprise." Bobby swept his light around, revealing wooden shelves and large metal cases, the dull green type that always had rocket launchers and that sort of thing in the movies. The yellow letters stamped on the sides in English indicated they held ammunition, grenades, and similar things. Several of the shelves had large silvery lumps of irregular material. They looked like mined ingots of raw metal. A tunnel led out of the chamber, running under the village. Shining the light down that way, it resembled an old mine shaft, the kind in abandoned gold mines in the movies.

Shining his light back on the metal cases, Bobby shrugged, "Reckon we oughta look through them all?"

"Yes. That seems like a very good idea." Stephen paced over and helped Bobby open them all, checking each one and finding most still had at least some of what the outside indicated they should. One was still completely full of explosives.

"Huh." Bobby straightened from the last case and shone his light down the tunnel again.

"You can say that again." Shutting and latching the last case again, Stephen also stood up. "At a guess, they found this ore and started mining it. When they sold it, someone decided it would be easier to just take it from them. Then our guys come in and find out they're using this metal and don't like the bad guys, so they trade for the metal and give them weapons to help them fight the good fight. Now someone wants to go back on that deal and just blast the town out of existence to take the metal."

"Yeah. You think telling Klein we found the stash on the second pass and destroyed it would work?"

"No, they'll just send troops in or do an air strike or something. Because it's got to be all about the metal ore."

This was a tough nut to crack, for sure. Metal would probably survive a bombing, so they had no incentive not to do it. Unless— "We could tell 'em we destroyed the weapons and found one little ingot of metal." He pointed to the smallest rock on the shelves, one only about the size of his fist. "They done got a tunnel and we followed it to the end and it's all exhausted of the metal, there ain't nothing here."

Stephen rubbed his chin thoughtfully, picked up the small rock. "It's heavy." It didn't burden him in any way. "Or we could tell Klein the truth, that they have this metal and are willing to sell it."

Bobby paced back to the hole. "Gimme a boost, we'll figure it out there. No reason to completely wreck these folks' evening."

Chuckling, Stephen paced over, rock securely in hand, and pretended to give Bobby a boost while actually tossing him up. In return, Bobby turned around reached down to give Stephen an unnecessary hand to get out. "We'll do what we can to prevent other Americans from coming here and being unreasonable," Stephen told the one man. "No one deserves to die over this." He lifted the one rock. "This may help us do that, is it alright if we take it?"

"Yes. Good." The interpreter shook hands with both of them. "Allah watch you."

CHAPTER 5

Stephen cracked his neck and pulled the headset out of his ear again. "I'm pretty sure they aren't going to torch the site." He stared at the rock, still in his hand. "I'll have to hand this over as proof. Klein seems like a decent guy who wants to get it right."

Bobby spent those five minutes chewing mechanically through another protein bar. "Seemed to me like a guy what's got overseers breathing down his neck, looking for results with not enough time to provide."

Nodding his agreement, Stephen pocketed the rock. "Let's move on to the second site. What do we need to do there?"

"Warlord," Bobby said with his mouth still half full. He swallowed the last bite before elaborating. "We're s'posed to scout his compound well enough to draw a map, check the security, and generally provide enough intel for a team to go in and take the guy out."

"Listen to you," Stephen smirked, "using grown-up military words like 'intel'."

Bobby snorted and stuffed his garbage away in a pocket. "Klein done said that if we got a good chance, and are okay doing it, we should just take the guy out, but I done told him to stuff that."

"Well," Stephen said thoughtfully, staring off into the darkness, "we'll see. If we catch him raping a twelve year old or something, I won't have a problem killing him."

One short hop later, they reached a city more modern in appearance than Bobby had expected to find in a constantly war-torn region. "What d'ya think?" They crouched behind some juniper bushes a block away from the compound, in the shadows of a smaller house. Neither of them was hidden terribly well, but anyone walking by would have to specifically look to see them.

"It's too easy."

"'Course it's easy. Nobody expects the Vampire-Dragon Inquisition."

Stephen blinked once and stared at Bobby. "I never would have figured you for a Monty Python fan."

"I got no idea what that's got to do with snakes, but I ain't 'specially keen on 'em."

"Okay." Stephen blinked again, shook that off, then went back to the matter at hand. "But, what I mean is, there isn't enough security for it to be what they said it is. They can't possibly think we're stupid enough to just go in, poke around, and hand over everything needed to kill a man."

Bobby shrugged, not sure he saw how Stephen reached that conclusion. "Maybe we played dumb better'n we thought."

The vampire raised an eyebrow and quirked one corner of his mouth up into a grin. "Perhaps. If we don't do this for them, though, they'll just go in without the quality information we could get them, and probably several people will get killed, including this man who may or may not be in need of killing."

"Well, okay. So now what?"

"I don't know."

Sighing lightly, Bobby rubbed his face. "I got an idea, but it ain't a good one."

Stephen snorted. "Where have I heard that before?"

"C'mon." Bobby chuckled. He tapped Stephen's shoulder as he stood and they walked together up to the front door.

"This is your brilliant plan?"

"Worked last time, didn't it?" They walked through the courtyard outside the house, past cameras that tracked them. Bobby resisted the urge to wave. When they reached the front door, he used the knocker shaped like a lion's head. "If somebody shoots first, we eat them."

"I am amenable to your plan."

"If'n that means you're up for it, then okay, good."

A dusky skinned man in a black suit opened the door and looked down his nose at them. "Can I help you?" He looked and sounded certain the answer would be 'No, sorry to bother you'. He also had a British accent, suggesting where he learned the language.

"We're looking to have a chat with Mr. Hanamidi, please."

The man looked at Bobby like he was a very strange creature, indeed. "Why do American soldiers want to speak with Mr. Hanamidi?"

"On account our boss says we gotta. You can tell him if he don't talk to us, a SEAL team'll probably be here sometime in the next few days to talk with bullets 'stead of words." In an effort to show his earnestness, he lifted his hands and unbuttoned his jacket to show he had no gun or explosives. With a light jab from his elbow, Stephen did the same.

The man looked them both over skeptically. "Wait here." He shut the door.

Bobby turned and waved at the cameras, and pulled his jacket off so they could see without a doubt that he had no weapon. "C'mon, play nice."

Stephen heaved a long suffering sigh and followed suit. "If they want us to pull down our pants, I'm going to be very unhappy."

"Me too." Grabbing a protein bar out of a pocket, Bobby ripped the package open and chomped it. "These things're awful."

"And yet, you eat them."

Looking down at the bar, he sighed, then swallowed the bite as quickly as possible. "Yeah. I s'pose it's better than a half-rotten apple from a dumpster."

"I've seen you eat those, too."

Nodding, Bobby took another bite. Just as he finished that and was about to stuff the rest of the bar into his mouth, the door opened again. The man in the suit gestured for them to come inside. "Mr. Hanamidi will see you." They followed him, Bobby tucking his 'food' into a pocket for later. It wasn't as nice on the inside as it seemed like it should be from the outside. Compared to that little village, though, this was a palace. It had hardwood floors, white walls and ceiling, and decent wood and metal furniture.

The butler led them a short way in and gestured to a small room with one couch and two chairs, some knickknacks on a coffee table, and bookshelves full of books along the walls. The person who must be Mr. Hanamidi stood at a bar on one end of the room, pouring amber liquid into a glass. "Would either of you like a drink?" He looked like the locals, with the proper dark olive skin tone, graying black hair and beard, and dark eyes, yet he sounded American. At a guess, Bobby would peg him as being in his 60s, maybe a well-aged 70.

"No, thanks," Bobby said as he sat down on the couch. Stephen shook his head and paced nonchalantly to a bookcase, where he started examining the contents. "I appreciate you seeing us, Mr. Hanamidi."

"The way you phrased your request was convincing." He waved to the butler and the man left them, pulling the door shut to give them privacy. Mr. Hanamidi brought his glass to one of the chairs opposite Bobby and sat down. At this point, he noticed Bobby's unusual icy blue, almond shaped eyes, and looked a bit longer than would generally be considered polite. He glanced at Stephen, but the vampire had his back to them. "I'm not surprised to know someone in the military wants to kill me, but I *am* surprised you both would warn me about it."

Stephen stepped to the next bookcase, still examining the titles. "As it turns out, their duly appointed assassins aren't really of a mind to just kill people for no reason."

"We noticed you ain't got a whole lotta security, and were kinda wondering if you might be able to tell us why the folks pulling our strings think you're a warlord what oughta be dead."

Hanamidi laughed. "Is that really what they told you?" Shaking his head with amusement, he snorted. "How pathetic it took them this long to find me. I assume you know nothing, then?"

"You assume correctly," Stephen said. "We'd like to learn."

"Mmm. Knowledge. It's a double-edged sword, often." Hanamidi took a sip of his drink and regarded it. "Do either of you know much about physics and the Theory of Relativity?"

"Nope, nothing." Bobby shrugged.

Stephen turned to regard Hanamidi, his brow raised. "Is this about time travel?"

"No, not exactly." Hanamidi looked at Bobby, apparently intending to direct the explaining at him. "My parents were Afghan, they wound up in Russia before I was born, where they both became scientists. When I was ten, they defected to America. It was a popular thing to do then, in certain circles. I studied physics, like my father, and went into government service, where I was tapped for a very sensitive project that had been going on for a long time already, some forty years. It was called Maze Beset."

Surprised by this unexpected connection, Bobby leaned in and nodded along. Stephen stopped pretending he had any interest in the books and stared openly at Hanamidi.

"Ah, so you know something more than nothing, then. What have you heard of the project?"

"We ran into Kurt Donner," Bobby explained, remembering the homeless man in El Paso. "He didn't tell us nothing more than the name. Then he keeled right over and died."

Shaking his head, Hanamidi said, "I don't know that name. He might have worked there at a different time or in a different part of the project. I was in Sierra Tango Alpha, STA, the Space-Time Anomaly section. The whole thing was so hush-hush that I only knew my partners. I saw other people around, but wasn't told anything about the other sections. They had data from what they asserted was an anomalous space-time event that occurred over Roswell, New Mexico in 1947. Our task was to recreate it somehow."

Stephen snorted. "Seriously? Roswell?"

"Yes, seriously." Hanamidi shrugged. "A weather balloon really did crash, but it wasn't the only thing to happen that day. I know very little about that—it was need to know and we were told we didn't need to know. What I do know is that the data I was working with was..." He took another drink, this one more than just a sip. "It made no sense in some ways. We were able to reproduce one part or another part, but never all at once. It was highly suggestive, though, of things that hadn't even been dreamed of when it first happened." His eyes lit up with interest. "So much of what we know now, in astrophysics specifically, and other branches of physics generally, came from the research done there, the experiments, the attempts."

"I don't know nothing about none of that," Bobby said slowly, frowning. "You recognize us a little, though, don't you? You kinda looked at the eyes."

Hanamidi took another swallow of his drink and sighed with nostalgia. "I saw a picture once. I wasn't supposed to see it. She was a beautiful creature, even in a black and white photo, but so sad. It was in a folder that a woman dropped and scattered the papers all over. I picked up the photo and she snatched it out of my hands without an explanation." His gaze unfocused. "Such haunting—and haunted—eyes."

"What'd they look like?" The answer seemed obvious, but Bobby had to ask the question, especially since Hanamidi didn't seem like he was going to snap out of his reverie any time soon without help.

Another tiny sigh escaped him and Hanamidi looked down at his rapidly depleting drink. "Just like yours." His gaze went to Stephen first, then Bobby. "Exactly like them, in fact. I'm not sure what color hers were, but I expect it was the same as yours, or quite similar to it. Her face was more angular, and the one ear I could see had a point at the top corner, but your eyes, they're hers. I have no idea who she was, but she must have had something to do with the Anomaly."

Stephen frowned through all of this, then finally shook his head. "She sounds like an elf."

Hanamidi chuckled. "I've seen some of the fantasy art. Yes, that is generally what she looked like: an elf. Less humanish than is typically portrayed, though." He shrugged. "In '95, they decided I was ready to retire and be replaced by a younger scientist who they could pay less. Someone tipped me off that my ability to enjoy my retirement would be rather shorter than I would like, so I fled back to my parents' homeland, knowing I could hide effectively here. Who knew the US would decide you could succeed where the Russians failed? Not I, certainly. And now, here you are at my door, telling me I have been found."

Bobby sighed heavily and rubbed his forehead with one hand. "I ain't here to kill nobody what I ain't gotta."

"We could just report back that we've done it and let you leave on your own."

"Don't be foolish," Hanamidi snorted. "They aren't stupid enough to let me walk out of here alive now that they know where I am. It's possible they sent you to flush me out, expecting you to let me go but hoping you'll be too stupid or thick to ask questions. After all, I'm an Afghan in Afghanistan who they labeled a 'warlord'; that should be enough for any red-blooded American boy to mindlessly kill me."

Uncomfortable with that statement, Bobby shifted in his seat and rubbed his face again, trying to figure a way out of this without anyone having to die. "We could get you out of here without anyone seeing it if the lights are turned off."

Hanamidi sighed and stared off at the wall again. Perhaps half a minute passed in silence, with Bobby and Stephen sharing a glance, then watching the other man. What might be going through his mind, Bobby had no idea. "Perhaps." He said it like someone asked him a question. His gaze snapped back to Bobby, intense and piercing. "If I give you some papers, would you swear to get them to my daughter?"

It was a weird question, and Bobby blinked, but also nodded. "Um, sure, soon as I could, yeah."

The scientist stood up abruptly. "Give me...ten minutes should be enough. Too much longer and they'll start to question what you were doing in here all this time." Without giving either of them a chance to respond, he left the room, his stride swift and purposeful.

Bobby watched him go, bewildered. "What in heckbiscuits was that?"

His mouth sliding downward into a grimace of distaste, Stephen shook his head. "Not sure, but I have a guess. Ten minutes strikes me as about enough time to put together a packet for his daughter to claim his assets, if his affairs are already in order, as they say."

Understanding what Stephen just hinted around the edges about took Bobby a minute. "You think he's going to tell us to kill him."

"Sometimes," Stephen sighed, "the best way to deal with something like this is to let it happen."

"That's—It ain't right is what it is." Bobby stood and wanted to throw something. Instead, he tucked his hands into his armpits and paced, kicking the couch as he went by. "I ain't no killer." The moment it left his mouth, he knew he'd just lied; he'd killed three men. Clinging to that made him a damned hypocrite. "I mean, not like this, not a-purpose-like, not because somebody told me to. Them, I killed because they were gonna do stuff to me or somebody else. This guy, he ain't doing nothing to nobody."

"Relax." Stephen sank into his chair, grimace turning to disgust. "You don't need to stain your hands, I'll do it. He won't even feel any pain."

Bobby froze and faced Stephen. "Shoot, I didn't mean it like that."

"No," Stephen smiled darkly, "I didn't think you did. But, the fact remains that I can do this and you don't have to."

"We could still sneak him out some—"

"It won't work. No matter how much you want it to, Bobby, it won't." Stephen snorted. "He's right: they're probably watching, they know we walked in through the front door, and once we report it's done, they'll find a way to make sure we weren't lying. That means there needs to be a body, and it needs to be his. Since neither of us has any way to generate a fake body, we need the real one."

"This is—" Kicking the couch again, Bobby couldn't settle on any one word to best fit there.

"Demented? Yes, but life is like that. Remember how I said this isn't going to be about right and wrong? Welcome to that world. We have to make choices and live with them. Our choice, the one to do their dirty work in the hopes we'd be able to get to Jasmine, set us up for this choice, and now we have to deal with it."

Jasmine's name felt like a slap in the face, and Bobby turned away to not have to look at Stephen's determination and gods-be-damned calm. This wasn't right, no matter how it got sliced or diced or blended. Noticing his belly rumbling again, he pulled out the last of that crappy bar and jammed it into his mouth. Really, he couldn't decide which thing bothered him most: that they were talking about killing someone, that Stephen was so unfazed by the idea, that he found himself hungry while talking about it, or that not killing Hanamidi might be worse overall than killing him.

"This sucks."

"I agree completely."

Someday, Bobby would be able to sit his ass down on a porch again and not have to deal with all this crazy crap. He'd drink a beer and watch the world drift by, knowing no one waited on his decision to save or damn them. Today wasn't that day. Tomorrow didn't look promising, either. "I guess maybe I oughta scrap with some of his people while you're...doing that."

He couldn't find it in himself to look at Stephen, so he just heard the vampire say, "That sounds like a good plan."

The door opened again, and Hanamidi walked in with determination written across every inch of his being. He offered Bobby a large envelope. "I'm not sure how to ask this. You've both been decent and reasonable."

Scowling, Bobby took the envelope. Tidy yet hasty letters on the manila paper gave them a destination in Albuquerque.

"Ah, I see you've figured it out, then." Hanamidi moved stiffly to the bar. "To you who are young, this probably seems strange, but I'm seventy-three and my wife passed a few years ago, I haven't seen my children since we fled without them. I don't even know how many grandchildren I have, if any. Living here, it's like half of a life." Shaking his head, he huffed out a not-quite-amused breath. "You know, I've thought a few times about saving everyone a lot of time, effort, and money by eating a bullet." He poured himself another glass of amber liquid and drank it down.

Stephen crossed the room with small, slow steps. "At least this way we were able to learn something that may eventually help us discover who we really are. If it helps to know, there will be no pain."

"I appreciate that."

Unwilling to stand there helplessly and watch, Bobby fled the room. He saw the butler standing in the hallway, leaning against the wall and staring, his face pale. "I've been with him since he got here," the man said. "He's a good man, a good employer. Like a brother."

Bobby squirmed as he walked over. This was not fair, it was not fun, and it was not right. He was going to do it anyway. "I gotta rough you up some," he said apologetically. "I ain't gonna do nothing that won't heal."

The butler looked up at Bobby and nodded. "That's a small mercy, I suppose, but I expect anyone who comes to verify his death will kill me. I'm too big a risk to be left alive."

Blanching, Bobby thought very hard about turning around and just walking away from this whole mess. "I ain't gonna do that. We could help you run for it, get you out far enough anyone watching can't just cut you down. A good shiner'd probably be a good idea still, though."

Much relieved, the butler nodded. "Yes, that might work. Thank you."

Tasting bile, Bobby scowled again as he made a fist with his right hand. "Dammit, don't thank me for doing this."

CHAPTER 6

Stephen reported in to Klein as they left the house, his face dark and brooding but a bounce in his step. They flew away, the vampire carrying the unconscious butler, and left him in an alley a few blocks away where the man claimed he should be safe enough for a few hours, long as they covered him with garbage. Bobby clenched his jaw the whole time they spent tending to the task in silence.

The pair took back to the air and went looking for the cave entrance. It was only a short hop, giving Bobby barely enough time to even deal with the facts of everything that just happened, let alone how he felt about it. Frequent glances at Stephen kept him from saying anything about it, worried, the vampire might need the silence.

They returned to the ground about a mile from the dot on the map, neither of them ready to tackle this situation. Bobby re-formed and shoved protein bars into his mouth to keep it busy while Stephen sat and stared into the darkness. Glancing at Stephen's watch, he saw the time: 11:32pm. Not even midnight, and they'd already finished two-thirds of their to-do list.

Bobby chewed and stared and stared and chewed. He hadn't done anything, except stand by and let his friend murder a man, and beat up another one for no reason. He listened to dry leaves scraping across the hard-packed earth in a light breeze and wondered if he'd left a piece of his soul behind in that house.

Beside him, Stephen pulled the envelope out of his pack and turned it over in his hands. He ran his fingers over the lettering on the front, then found it unsealed and peered inside. Sliding the thick stack of papers out, he held them so Bobby could see, too.

The top page began Hanamidi's last will. Several pages under that appeared to be legal documents of one kind or another. Next, they found pictures, both loose and mounted on scrapbook pages. Stephen flipped through them, showing all family and kids' school pictures. The rest of the papers had scribbled notes in Arabic with drawn diagrams. Some boasted coffee stains.

Tucking the stack back into the envelope, Stephen said, "I wonder what kind of space-time anomaly it was."

"I wonder if anyone at the farm'll be able to understand any of this stuff."

"I also wonder how long it'll be before we can get back there, and if we'll be relieved of all these documents before then."

Pleased to discuss anything other than what happened to Hanamidi, Bobby scratched at the few days of beard on his chin. "Maybe we oughta mail 'em."

"Maybe. That would mean a mailman would have to go there, though, which might be counter-productive."

Bobby grunted to concede the point. If only Hannah had a Post Office box set up someplace, but why would they do that? To make sure they could get lingerie catalogs? "We could mail it to Kris."

"We could mail it to Adesha," Stephen tapped the address already on the envelope.

"I dunno." As good as the idea sounded, Bobby figured there had to be a downside, even if he couldn't think of it. "If mailing something to her was all what needed to be done, Hanamidi coulda done that anytime."

Stephen grunted to acknowledge the point. "I don't want to involve Kris in anything she can't back out of yet."

"I guess the best choice right now is to hold onto it all. S'pose if'n we gotta, we could stash it someplace and come back later."

Nodding, Stephen tucked the envelope into his pack again. For several seconds, they sat in silence again. "It felt really good."

Bobby shifted with discomfort. He looked down at his hand and made a fist, remembering the satisfaction he felt for a flash when it connected with that man's face. "Mmm." He wanted to deny it until it went away. Stephen deserved better from him. Covering his mouth, he coughed. "It was kinda scary how much I really needed to beat the crap outta someone."

Stephen picked up a dead leaf and crumpled it in his hand, then let it fall to the ground. "I've fed before, plenty of times, but I've never killed anyone doing it. Gotten close, but never all the way to death. Killing Hanamidi, it was like really great sex, and part of me wants to do it again. Not right this minute. I'm completely sated right now, but I can feel how it'll be harder to stop myself the next time I feed. It's like..."

He stared out at the darkness, breathing slow and even and deep. "Like having chocolate for the first time. You've had ice cream, cake, maybe cookies before that, but then you get to have chocolate, pure and perfect, and nothing else is ever as good."

Bobby didn't have that kind of feeling towards any particular kind of food. He got the idea anyway. "You don't know that."

"Yes, I do. It's the same difference as between having a little snack and draining them to unconsciousness. I can stop, but why should I? Every pint past the first tastes better than the one before, and that last one, when I had to suck it out instead of letting it dribble into my mouth, it was like pure fucking ambrosia. If I hadn't felt it coming on, I would've made a mess of my pants."

That kind of admission had to be tough to make. Bobby couldn't relate to it. Sure, he got a rush out of beating that guy up. For him, it had been nothing more than a way to exorcise some frustration, and had nothing to do with sex or pleasure. On top of that, he'd felt... It confused him, because he went out of control, but while it happened, he'd thought he had total control.

He flexed his hand and wondered if some of that came from the dragons. "Thanks for stopping me. Sorry I couldn't do the same for you."

Stephen nodded, still staring off at nothing. "We were so worried about Matthew. We're just as dangerous as he is."

Sitting around brooding got them exactly two places: no and where. Bobby breathed in deeply, wanting to shake off the impulse to be horrified at the pair of them. What could he do about that? Not be himself anymore? Somehow kill Stephen? "We just gotta do what we can to fight it." The absurdity of his statement made him huff. "C'mon, though. Night ain't getting longer."

"Yeah." Stephen rubbed his eyes and got up by virtue of floating until he could unfold and put his feet on the ground. "I can control this. I'm the one in control, not the Hunger. It can go fuck itself off a short pier with a dead armadillo." He set off across the rocky steppe, paying attention to his footing.

Bobby struggled with that mental picture, then shook it off as unimportant and flowed into the swarm to avoid tripping over anything. A handful of dragons landed on Stephen's shoulders and the rest swirled around behind him.

A quick glance to one side then the other made Stephen smirk and hum a tune that Bobby recognized as 'Enter Sandman'. If it related somehow, he didn't understand. Regardless, the vampire allowed the dragons to stay, which made them happy. They seemed to like Stephen, in a different way than they liked Sebastian. Maybe a better word for it was 'respect'. He thought the kind of respect a body gave to a tiger was more appropriate, but he didn't have much say over what they thought. Which was demented, of course, since they were him and he was them.

Despite efforts made to camouflage it, Stephen easily found the entrance to the cave they'd come looking for. A few shrubs and creative door placement didn't defeat the vampire's senses. "There are definitely people in there someplace," he said softly. "I can...tell." That wasn't at all the word he was going to say at first.

Right then, for the first time, he wondered if he could re-form only enough of himself to speak, and what that would look like, and how it would feel. He imagined a disembodied mouth being held up by a bunch of dragons. If he could shudder at the thought, he would have.

Stephen took the disguised handle and gave it a little yank. Two animal hides had been lashed together in a wood frame decorated by sprigs of plant material. When it had opened a tiny crack, Bobby heard a jangling noise like a bunch of small metal things hitting each other came from the inside, and Stephen swore under his breath. "So much for the element of surprise," he muttered. Ripping the door off because he could, he tossed it for distance and strode inside. "Time for Plan B. Go ahead and scout the place in clumps, confuse whoever you find, and lead me to whatever I need to deal with."

This plan sounded a lot like all their other plans so far, giving Bobby no reason to object. He sent the dragons inside, choosing to see this as an opportunity to get more comfortable with his ability. The swarm flowed around Stephen, then down the earthen tunnel. It had just enough space for one person to walk, two if they were really friendly. It twisted and turned, and within half a minute, Bobby found the small room where the door chime must have been before Stephen pulled it out, along with the door.

Two men lurched to their feet from crate chairs with woven blankets falling to the floor from their laps. They looked how he expected terrorist-types to look, which reminded him of those folks in that first village. Those men had been ordinary folks, doing what they could to protect and feed their families. He saw one major difference: those people lived above ground, and these people lived under it. Otherwise, they all had the same clothes, the same weapons, and the same general appearance.

That village turned out alright, giving him pause. Klein had called Hanamidi a warlord, and he'd said that village needed to be wiped out. Both had been one hundred percent wrong. Without any evidence of these people doing something they oughtn't to, attacking them struck Bobby as fulfilling the monster label. He wanted to grumble, because he had no idea how to tell the good guys from the bad guys if everybody looked the same.

Stephen would react to whatever those two men did, and Bobby had no particular reason to interfere. He could spook them, in the hopes they'd take pause and not get violent the second they saw him. The swarm spilled into the room, spreading out and filling it. The two men freaked in a foreign language and tried to bat away the dragons. Fortunately, neither had a taser or anything like it, and neither tried to shoot the swarm. It meant Bobby could keep the dragons from hurting the two men.

"I'll take it from here, Bobby, keep going." Stephen appeared in the tunnel mouth and shooed the swarm away. The dragons withdrew, and as they did, Stephen moved in and beat on the two men, putting them down without killing them. It may have happened by accident, but the vampire didn't rip anyone's body parts off or throw them too hard. He did, however, pick up a rifle and look it over.

One dragon stayed behind and perched on his shoulder again. Bobby figured he could use it to lead him when he had a reason to. The rest of the swarm found branches off the main tunnel and explored them. He found other men along the way and avoided them by flying fast and along the ceiling.

He flowed through a labyrinth of curves and unexpected drops and ladders into upper chambers, all lit at irregular intervals with bare light bulbs on what might be a continuous wire. Evidence of human effort in the digging out was minimal, mostly limited to rounding corners or enlarging individual chambers, and perhaps joining a few here and there. Some had generators chugging away, the wires from the lights connected to them, small holes shooting out from those spots to the outside. He found a few computers and plenty of weapons caches.

It felt big enough that fully exploring it would take months. He had the dragons splinter again and again to follow the various tunnels until they flitted about in groups of nine or ten. His mind floated around between them, getting the input from all their tiny eyes at once and painting a picture of a female-free zone focused on survival above anything else.

In one deep, dark, dank chamber that smelled of sweat and waste, a group of dragons freaked out until he focused on one and found five men in partial US military uniforms, all hog tied, gagged, and lying on the floor. He quashed his first impulse: getting the dragon on Stephen's shoulder to goad him into trashing the place to reach them. Until he knew whether these soldiers still lived or not, he saw no point to rushing through.

Instead, he flowed his mind into one of the dragons there and looked around. One guard sat nearby, smoking a cigarette with a paperback book and a gun. The book had characters on the cover that Bobby assumed must be Arabic, though he'd never seen text of it before. As he watched the guard turn a page, obviously absorbed by the text, it occurred to him that dead bodies didn't need guards.

He flew the dragons down, avoiding getting into the guard's peripheral vision, and landed on the man farthest from the guard. His skin felt warm and his chest moved in the even rhythm of sleep or unconsciousness. This close, he could make out the others breathing, too.

With only five dragons—the number currently present—Bobby had no confidence he could handle a single guard on his own. If he could free these men, though, and they were capable enough, that would give him time to bring down the rest of the swarm, then these men could follow him as they fought their way back to meeting up with Stephen. He'd had worse ideas.

While the swarm changed direction to converge on the spot, these five dragons landed on the one soldier's legs and arms. They chomped on the rope bindings, using their sharp little teeth to saw the fibers away. The last few strands snapped and the soldier slumped, making Bobby freeze. When nothing happened, they moved to the next one.

This soldier, who appeared to be about Bobby's age, had no major, grievous injuries. On the way to the next, he had his one dragon fly up and down his body, checking, and he found a black eye, a split lip, and some purplish bruises on his bare feet. His plain gray shirt had smears of dried blood and minor rips with older bruises showing through. His camouflage pants appeared to be intact, aside from the mud and blood staining them.

All four of the others had received similar treatment. The oldest one by Bobby's estimation had cuts and bruises on the bottoms of his swollen feet. At a guess, he'd been tortured, maybe for being the highest ranking man among them, or just the one who resisted the most.

Rage simmered in the dragons. Though soldiers had been the enemy at Hill, he still considered them overall to be the good guys, especially here. Seeing them treated this way pissed him off. Whatever his feelings on the subject, though, he sternly reminded the dragons that five couldn't do anything useful to that guard, because they wanted to go rip him to bits. Freeing the rest of these men should at least distract them long enough for the swarm to gather.

None of the soldiers woke while he worked. All five had been freed by the time the swarm converged on the dark, empty space between the open doorway and the ladder up. He had the five dragons slip around to the rest of the swarm and re-formed, concerned about them going berserk. Without using them, though, he only had the element of surprise.

He took a deep breath, then rushed the guy. Unafraid of hurting himself, he slammed his body into the guard's and knocked him against the wall. The guard took the impact with a grunt, his eyes bulging. Both the book and the nearby assault rifle fell to the floor with a clatter. Bobby threw a solid punch across his jaw, kicked him in the gut, and stomped on his head.

Before he could get carried away this time, the dragons burst out of their own accord and fell upon the man, little claws scraping, little mouths blasting tiny jets of fire. The guard rasped and gurgled and mewled, all of it goading the swarm into a frenzy. When they finished killing the guy, Bobby got control back and re-formed standing beside the grisly corpse.

Staring down at what his swarm had done, Bobby swallowed down the urge to throw up. This time, he'd done it on purpose, except that he'd really done it to save those soldiers. That guard deserved to die for whatever part he'd had in cutting up the one soldier's feet. He nodded to himself, sure in the truth of it.

When he looked up, he found five pairs of eyes staring at him. Though he could see all around as the swarm, they'd been so focused on the guard that he hadn't noticed them waking up. For a few beats, he stood there with no idea what to say. The weight of their eyes made him squirm, so he raised a hand and cut through the air with it in an unenthusiastic wave.

"Hi. I'll be your rescue today."

All five had cloth gags Bobby hadn't messed with. The one in the back discovered they'd been freed and reached up to pull his gag out. "What *are* you, man?"

Bobby pursed his lips and dropped his gaze to the ground. That left him looking at the mangled body. He frowned, then he shrugged. Right now, they needed to get out of here, and him fussing about the state of his immortal soul wouldn't accomplish that. "The guy what's getting you out of here, that's what." He offered the nearest man a hand to help him to his feet. "You guys hurt, or just roughed up a bit?"

The man with the cut up feet recovered from the shock of Bobby first. He pulled his gag out and hefted a foot to take a look at it. "I don't think I can walk." He kept his voice low, yet Bobby could hear command in it, that certain something his daddy always had that made other people listen. "We're all that's left of our unit, the ones that weren't hurt or killed in the initial skirmish. Don't know what they did with the rest."

Nodding along as the man spoke, Bobby backed off and went to the doorway to see if he'd attracted any attention. No one had popped their head down or called out, so he turned back. They rubbed their wrists and ankles, and generally needed some vacation. "Y'all look like hell. I ain't much with a gun, so you guys should grab whatever he's got," he jerked a thumb at the dead guard, "but let me and my buddy do most of the work." At this point, he had the one loose dragon lead Stephen in.

"'Your buddy'? Is that a freaky way to refer to...um—"

"No. That'd be a 'them', not a 'he'. I mean I ain't alone. Brought me a vampire to help out." Rather than take the time to explain that, he sent a handful of dragons to scout it ahead. Behind him, the five men quietly freed themselves the rest of the way, searched the guard, and figured out how to get the one injured man out of here. Paying more attention to his scouts than the soldiers, he didn't hear if they said anything about him or a vampire, but figured they'd probably decided he must be insane.

Whatever they thought, these guys had their heads screwed on right. Two men hefted the injured one up and the other two had the guard's two guns between them. With their faces set in grim determination, these men obviously would do whatever it took to get out, and Bobby knew he had to take the same attitude if he wanted them all to survive.

"I'm gonna do whatever I can to keep you from having to use those to get outta here. Just so you know." Taking the lead, he approached the ladder and wondered at the best way to get the injured man up it.

The dragons wanted to dive in and take more of these men down with a disturbing level of eagerness. Bobby pressed on his forehead, trying to make them understand that one scream would make this much harder, and so would gunfire. Getting shot wouldn't help, either, and neither would senseless rampaging.

His solo dragon let him know that Stephen waltzed through the place, leaving a trail of bodies in his wake. They might be unconscious. Bobby watched the vampire grab two men and smash their heads together as he breezed past. They might have survived that, and he chose not to have his one dragon investigate. Some things, he figured, should be left unknown as long as possible.

Bobby peered up the ladder, knowing they'd find men up there, playing cards. His handful of dragons reported that nothing had changed. He held up a hand, put a finger to his lips, pointed up, and showed five fingers. They could wait for Stephen here, though it felt cheap and cowardly.

While he concentrated on what the dragons saw, one of the soldiers tapped him on the shoulder and leaned in to whisper to him. "We can lure one or two down here and ambush them. I speak the language."

Finding the plan better than anything he'd come up with so far, Bobby nodded. "The other choices are waiting for my partner to reach us, or making lots of noise."

The soldier frowned at that and flicked his eyes back to the rest of the group. He nodded and led Bobby to the huddled group. They welcomed him to join with only a sidelong glance or two. "Sarge, we can set up an ambush, wait for cavalry, or go guns blazing."

'Sarge' was apparently the one with the cut up feet. "Ambush for as long as we can, then switch to guns blazing. We're here, we should take advantage of that fact to take this base out."

"That ain't really my mission." The moment the words came out of his mouth, he knew them to be a complete lie. Klein said it would be 'full of traps'. He never used words out loud that demanded the deaths of everyone inside. His meaning had been clear, though, and Bobby had been stupid not to realize the true purpose of the mission. Obviously, they had been sent to verify the cave was full of bad guys, then kill them or make it easier for someone else to kill them.

He wasn't cut out for this stuff. For the first time, with his eyes on Sarge, Bobby realized that his daddy's job had been, more or less, killing people and not being bothered by it. How so many managed to handle it seemed more unbelievable than how many fell apart like Matthew. Clenching his jaw, Bobby nodded. "But let's do this. Call up for them whenever you're ready and I'll take care of it." He broke apart into the swarm and surrounded the ladder hole, spread out in the darkness and ready to engulf whoever dropped down into the trap.

The soldier called out with a request of some kind. Bobby heard the men upstairs mutter to each other. A chair scraped on the floor and one squatted beside the ladder hole. He called out in response and the soldier answered him. The man grumbled and climbed down the ladder.

Bobby waited until he had reached the ground and taken two steps away from the ladder. Dragons flung themselves at his face, intending to do tiny acts of violence to his eyes and neck. The man opened his mouth and one dove inside, shooting down his throat to shut him up. It reminded Bobby of digging around in Dan's shoulder to get that bullet out back in Salt Lake.

Killing a man happened to be easier from the inside than the outside. Bobby didn't want to re-form after the dragon on the inside burst out through the man's chest, mostly because he feared he'd throw up, which wouldn't help anything right now. The dragons, though, found the new knowledge invigorating. They shoved Bobby aside to get the job done, surging through the hole and diving at all four men at the table at once.

Streaking back through the place, the dragons went wild, gleefully forcing themselves down throats in small groups and bursting out through chests and stomachs. They found Stephen, who watched dragons explode out of two men with a stony expression, one he couldn't read. Not that he cared. Bobby managed to wrest control back and re-formed on all fours, violently heaving up what little had been in his stomach.

"I see you found something worthy of killing all these men," Stephen said as he crouched down beside Bobby, offering the canteen. His words came out gentle, without judgment.

Taking the water, Bobby spat out bile, then sat back up on his heels. His mouth tasted horrible. A mouthful of water swished around and spat out helped that. "They were holding some soldiers, five. Back thataway." He jerked a thumb to indicate the direction.

Stephen nodded. "Give me a dragon to lead me, and I'll meet you outside."

"All them on the way here dead already?"

The vampire's mouth went thin. "Yes. I assumed the dragon getting all excited meant I should."

"Yeah. Okay." He popped a dragon off his thumb, and it whirred off with instructions to show Stephen where to find the soldiers. Bobby got up and stumbled to the entrance, hand on the wall to steady himself and trying not to look as much as possible. He kept going until the cool air outside slapped him aside. Falling to his knees, he clutched his face with both hands. "What'd I do?"

He could feel them, the weight of their tiny minds pressing on his. They didn't understand. "A life is a life," he said aloud, trying to explain to them because he knew they could hear it, and he didn't feel coherent trying to think it at them. "I ain't saying these guys didn't deserve to die, but we ain't s'posed to be judge, jury, and executioner all at once. It ain't right to just take it all in our hands. Claws."

He pushed his hands up and through his hair, winding up with them grabbing the hair at the nape of his neck and tugging on it. "I'm the one in charge, you hear? Y'all are part of me, I ain't just another bit of you! I'm made of dragons, you're parts of me. You do what I tell you, not whatever you want."

His arms dropped to his sides and he stared up at the impossibly starry sky. It looked about the same here as at the farm. Maybe it was different, but not enough that he could tell. Right now, he should be there, not here. No one there would ask him to kill anyone. Not only would they not think he would in the first place, but if they did, they'd actually ask him not to kill anybody. How many men did he murder in that cave? He had no idea, and no intention of going back to count.

How was he supposed to look anyone in the face now, most especially himself? He had to remember that he came here for Jasmine, for all eleven of the ones they couldn't save. This was for them, because he and Stephen were sure if they could just get the damned suits to trust them, they could find out where those eleven had been taken and get them out. There wasn't supposed to be all this killing, wasn't supposed to be anything like this. When Privek said they'd be doing missions, he thought it would be a lot of spying, watching people and reporting back and not thinking. So stupid, he was so stupid. Both of them were monsters. Privek saw that and deployed them accordingly.

"I gotta be in control. I'm the person here. Y'all are just little pieces of me, and ought to act like it. Nobody else dies on account of me 'less I say so, and that's that." Until he could be sure they'd listen to him, he was a danger to anyone around him, even those soldiers, but he had no idea what to do about that. He heaved a heavy, despairing sigh and got to his feet, keeping his back to the cave entrance.

"I should report in," he heard Stephen say. Bobby's dragon trilled and zoomed over to reattach to his thumb. "Can I get your names and ranks to let them know who we have?"

"Buffalo Soldiers Sergeant Riker and Privates Hansen, Carson, Platt, and Hegi. Tell them like that. The rest of our unit is dead, so far as we know." Bobby recognized Sarge's voice.

Feet slapping the earth filled the silence that must have been Stephen putting on and activating the earpiece. "Cant and Mitchell reporting in. The cave has been cleared, we found five men." He relayed the names, as Riker told him to, then paused. Bobby glanced back to see Stephen carrying Riker on his back. The other four looked around, maybe just happy to be outside, maybe trying to unsee all those gruesome dead bodies. None of them looked at him, he could tell that much for sure. "Yes, Riker is injured, they're all beat up and probably dehydrated. We don't have enough water to walk through this come daylight, but we'll get as far south as we can."

"You heard the man," Riker barked. "Move out."

"Bobby, let's go."

He sighed again and stayed staring off into the darkness. "I'm thinking maybe I shouldn't oughta go back."

"I will admit the cave is nice and cozy, but the decorating isn't to my taste, and it's definitely a fixer-upper." Stephen left a short pause, then dropped the jovial tone. "At least walk with us, Bobby. We can talk later."

Rubbing his chin, Bobby nodded. "Yeah, I reckon." He turned and followed along behind the others, trying not to think much. His belly started to rumble angrily within a minute, and he bolted two of those gross protein bars without tasting them. As he stuffed the second wrapper in his pocket, it occurred to him that he maybe ought to offer the other bars to these guys. Then again, they seemed alright, and it would probably be better for them to get real food instead of this crap.

"Is it okay to ask..." One of the four Privates said it tentatively, and the statement hung there without him finishing it.

"No, it's really best if you don't," Stephen answered. "It would be even better if you forget we exist. Because we don't. We're figments of your imagination to be redacted from any retelling of this event that only sort of happened."

"Understood," Riker said. "Whatever happened in that little base, we didn't see it. Hansen wasn't tied up very well and managed to free himself, at which point we discovered we were clear to leave. Anyone have a problem with that?"

"Why's it gotta be Hansen?"

"I got double jointed thumbs." Hansen held up his hands and demonstrated the unusual way he could bend his thumbs. "All of you owe me your freedom," he grinned, "because without me, you'd have all starved to death down there."

From there, they fell to joking. Bobby listened in and couldn't figure out how they could see all that and move on so effortlessly. Maybe it had to do with their lack of involvement in the...butchering. They'd probably seen a ton of gruesome bodies before. Beyond that, freedom had to taste plenty good enough to ignore it all. As he'd done several times already, he rubbed his face with both hands. Imagining what Momma would say about all this didn't help in the slightest. Substituting Lily in there made things worse.

The thp-thp-thp of a helicopter nearing jarred him out of brooding and he looked up to see the lit up bird dropping down nearby. The soldiers rushed while Bobby slowed. He stopped dead a good forty paces away, watching two of the men climb in and help Stephen get Riker up and strapped in. Stephen turned and noticed Bobby. The vampire rolled his eyes and nodded to get Bobby to join them.

That look, the one that suggested Stephen considered it stupid for him to hang back, made him move. He couldn't say why, exactly, but his feet jogged over and he grabbed on. The helicopter lifted off without waiting for him to sit down or strap in. That was fine. If he fell, he'd just fly alongside. In a lot of ways, hanging out felt good, like someone blasted him with sand to scour away a layer of him, the layer that couldn't handle it all.

Did he want to be that guy? The one who could do something like that and move on? Was it enough that they deserved it? Did they 'deserve' it? What right did he have to judge something like that? He could only wonder if men like Klein thought about all the lives they ordered others to take for some greater good, if pondering whether he'd done the right thing kept him awake at night.

About an hour later, the bird set down in a smaller camp than Klein's. It had most of the same features, and Bobby forced himself to follow his nose to the food. He ate mechanically until his belly filled, then found a rock to sit on and stare at nothing. Orange and pink announced the impending sunrise, and he watched it climb up over the horizon.

By all rights, he ought to be tired. His mind buzzed with the things he'd seen and done in that cave, from the first corpse to the last, and all their innards. Some of those things, he'd never wanted to know what they actually looked like, because they belonged on the inside. Of course, that bothered him a lot less than the rest of it.

"Do you want to talk about it?" Stephen's voice, muffled by the cloth protecting his face from the sunshine, came from behind him.

"I ain't even got any blood on me. I oughta have a little, a few smudges or something."

"I expect all the stains are on the inside."

Bobby had no answer for that. He scratched his chin, the stubble rasping against his fingertips.

"I reported in, Klein is ecstatic. As part of the report, I informed him we aren't interested in continuing to pursue these sorts of missions. He pouted, but said he'd pass that along."

"How d'ya know he pouted?"

Stephen chuckled lightly. "Don't tell me you've never heard anyone pout over the phone."

The slight change of subject brought out a bare hint of a smirk. "Can't say as I have. Had girls roll their eyes at me over the phone, though."

"This is sort of like that, only more amusing to listen to." The vampire let silence hang between them as he moved closer and sat on the next rock. "I won't lie to you, Bobby. You scare the crap out of me. I can kill people pretty easily, but only one, maybe two at a time. Right now, I'm wondering if you could kill me by crawling down my throat and ripping your way out. A massive amount of damage? I might not be able to heal that before I bleed out. I'm not actually afraid of you, though, because I know you'd never try it unless I needed to be put down."

Nodding, Bobby tried not to take it as a stinging indictment. "Did those men need to be put down?"

"I really don't know. I'm fairly certain that, if given the chance, they would've tried to kill us. They would've failed, though, so I can't say where the balance there is. Is it justified to kill someone who shoots me? What if he only points the gun? How about if I only know he would but kill him before he can? Does that really make either of us any better than paranoid serial killers? I just have no idea."

He paused and took a deep breath, letting it out slowly. "I do know this is a war zone, and in war, it's us against them. No matter who's right or just more right, we have to pick a side. Staying neutral back home is fine, but staying neutral out here isn't possible. We chose us, so they want to kill us, and out here, that means we kill them first so they can't kill any of us. It sucks, but that's war."

That did pretty well sum up the whole situation. "You think I'm being a whiny pansy-ass twit."

"No," Stephen laughed, "I think you're being human. But then, we aren't really human, are we?"

No, they sure weren't human. If this whole thing didn't show him that, nothing could. "We back out now and they're gonna come after us."

"Probably. I propose that if our request to be utilized differently is refused, we make for Albuquerque to meet Hanamidi's daughter. From there, Roswell is probably the next stop."

"We should go back to the farm and get reinforcements for Roswell."

"Or send someone else, yes, good point."

"There probably ain't nothing in Roswell, though." Glad for the true change of subject, Bobby thought about it. "I mean, they got tourist stuff there. It'd be kinda dumb to keep a secret base or whatever in a place what gets so much traffic."

"Yes," Stephen nodded thoughtfully, "it's more likely to be in some kind of Area 51."

Huffing out a light snort, Bobby shook his head and grinned. "That ain't really real, is it?"

Also amused, Stephen smirked. "It's probably not called that, but yes, I assume we have at least one secret installation somewhere that pursues projects best kept away from public opinion." Gloved fingers of one of his hands drummed idly on his knee. "You know, I'm curious why they decided to put us out in the real world instead of doing this whole thing as a controlled experiment. It would have been easier to get us to do whatever they want if we were all raised to just be soldiers."

That notion hadn't coherently occurred to Bobby, but now Stephen said it out loud, he agreed. "Momma said she was part of a program, they helped her clean herself up. Lots of women were in it, though, and she was the only one what got knocked up that she knew of. Maybe..." The gears turned in his head as things fell into place and made more sense than they had before. "She said it was still a new process then. What if that was the best way they could think of to try lots of times? I mean, look, we're all from all over the country, right?

"Momma was born and raised in Atlanta, she ain't never left much, and didn't say nothing about going far away for that testing stuff. I got the feeling Lizzie and Dan ain't never been outta Arkansas, Javier and Tiana was from LA, Alice was from San Francisco, and on and on. So, say they done did this in lots of places, hid it as a 'social program' on account they were helping women. Heck, it mighta even been part of the war on drugs stuff. Momma said they offered to get me adopted, but she said no. Maybe the ones what the momma decided to keep 'em, they couldn't do nothing about. Maybe it weren't something they thought about before starting the program.

"But more, what if they didn't have no idea what we'd turn into? If they didn't know if it would rightly work, maybe they didn't know what would happen when it did work. Momma also said they told her to watch for 'anything unusual'. She thought they meant sickness. *Maybe they did mean sickness, and this was a big surprise.* Ain't none of us got picked up until recent-like, and all of us started having superpowers around the same time. What if...what if they picked the four of us—me, Jayce, Alice, and Ai —by random offa that list because one of us what got their superpower came to their attention already by then?"

Stephen kept his mouth shut, letting Bobby ramble until he finished. "We're all in a small age range, eighteen to twenty-two. They may have had to cut something because of funding issues, and chosen our program, viewing it as a failure. This is all just guessing, though, Bobby. It could be a lot more sinister than you think."

He had a point. Bobby shook his head anyway. "You know, I didn't do so hot in school or nothing, but it seems to me that most of the time in the real world when science gets used like this, it's less 'I wanna take over the world' and more 'I wanna see what happens'."

"Fair point. But where did they get the DNA they crossed with human to wind up with us?"

"No clue." He shrugged and snorted. "Maybe there really were aliens in Roswell."

"Anything is possible, I suppose, though I wonder how it really got here. If there was actually a spacecraft, I would expect our space program to be a little farther along by now." Cocking his head to one side, Stephen held up a hand to stop the conversation, then put a hand to his ear to activate the mic. "Yes, Klein, I'm here." He listened, then sighed. "Just a minute, let me confer with Bobby." He turned off the mic again. "We were so efficient, they want to appeal to our desire to be patriotic Americans and to save the lives of more soldiers by pursuing other dangerous missions that would likely involve a lot of killing."

Unsurprised, Bobby scratched the back of his neck and stretched. Riker and his men had probably been written off as killed in action before he and Stephen rescued them. That whole cave now held dead bodies instead of presumed terrorists. Hanamidi was dead. A suspected weapons cache had been emptied. They did their job well, and Uncle Sam liked soldiers who did their job well. Really, he couldn't blame them. Weapons like them changed the course of history. "They ain't never gonna let us leave until this thing is done here. We wanna stay and end this damned war, this here's our chance."

Stephen shrugged. "I have to admit there's some allure to that. A lot of good people have died here." He paused and turned to fix Bobby with a stare, though his sunglasses made that unclear. "We should decide together, though, not separately. I have a feeling that there will come a point when I don't remember why it matters anymore. They'll drag me down into a pit until I become the monster inside and nothing more. Having someone here with me should help prevent that."

"But you wanna stay?" Bile rose up in Bobby's throat. He swallowed hard to push it back down where it belonged.

"Not exactly. I like knowing that Riker, if he has a brother or a sister, a wife, whatever, they didn't lose him. Because of me."

"Hm." The question, then, was how much he, Bobby, could stomach. If he looked at it as saving American lives, could he be okay with taking some Afghan kid's big brother or dad away instead? Both of them stared out at the nothing, as if the rocks and scrub would have answers. "Tell 'em... Shoot, I dunno. Right and wrong is all screwed up out here. Which is more important—saving soldiers' lives or finding the missing eleven?"

"Yeah, I don't know, either." Stephen hung his head and shrugged. "If we save twenty lives, is that worth those eleven? I'm not used to tackling truly difficult moral issues. Up to now, I've been going based on killing and rape being bad, the Hunger's wishes notwithstanding. I didn't really need more nuance than that."

One of them had to make a decision. "Tell 'em—" Bobby rubbed his face again and sighed. "Tell 'em we're on board. Privek ain't gonna trust us with nothing if we bail now. We gotta at least try. If'n it means we gotta kill more, then, well, I guess." He rubbed his eyes, finally tired enough to sleep.

Nodding his agreement, Stephen moved his hand to talk to Klein again. "I can live with that. Can you?"

Bobby grimaced. "I already got forty-some bodies on my tab. What's forty more?"

"Maybe we should get some sleep, because that actually sounded funny."

"A-damned-men."

ASIDE – LIAM

Liam hated his job. Nothing else could be worse and he had no choice. Three weeks of this crap so far. Three weeks since Elena disappeared. Three weeks since his world fell apart. They'd find her. He only needed to do something in return, so they could justify the man-hours. Oh, sure, he tried to pay them off. His father had more than enough money to cover those salaries. That bastard Privek wanted something else.

Gritting his teeth, he laid a hand on the unconscious soldier's bare thigh. At the ankle, this leg ended in a mass of blood-stained gauze. Under that, he knew he'd find a ragged end, treated enough to prevent the victim from bleeding out. No one told him what happened to his patients, and he didn't ask because he didn't want to know.

Doing this meant serving his country, he'd been told, as if that would make everything better. He took a deep breath and braced himself. With a twist and a pull someplace inside, he did the impossible and clamped down on a scream as the injury transferred from the soldier's leg to his own. Blood gushed out of Liam's ankle and flesh wrapped itself around the soldier's.

His thrice-damned power created miracles at the cost of his sanity.

An eternity of agony later, the soldier still had no foot, but his leg ended in a smooth, healed and rounded stump. They'd be able to fit him with a fake foot now, there would be no oozing and weeping and pus, and the guy could avoid the potential problem of addiction to pain meds. Liam glared at the man for the crime of putting him through a few minutes of hell.

Reaching down, he swiped the blood off his already regenerated foot with a towel. The second he'd seen the injury, he'd pulled his combat boot and sock off and set them aside. His assistant swooped in with her mop and sloshed the blood off the plastic under him for the thousandth time since he got here. She'd gotten good at it, and took only two swishes before she wordlessly wheeled the soldier's gurney out. He'd wake up later and be confused, and someone would tell him to thank God, or his lucky stars, or whatever, and to not ask questions. He'd be walking again by nightfall if they had any prosthetics handy.

Before he had a chance to put his sock back on, two soldiers carried a third in. Another pair peered inside the tent. All five—curiously barefoot and stained, bloodied, and half-dressed by camp standards—had been banged up, but Liam didn't treat bruises and cut lips. He dealt with serious injuries. His patients either avoided months to years of surgeries and rehab, or they went back out into the field as a result of his ministrations.

He might have shooed them out, except the man they carried had serious foot injuries. They'd been cut and smashed and generally mis-treated to the point of uselessness. Torture did things like that, he sup-posed. If this guy wound up being able to walk after it healed normally, he'd have pain for the rest of his life. For whatever reason, they hadn't cut off any of his toes. Maybe he'd escaped or been rescued before they got that far.

Standing with a sigh, he vacated his stool and gestured for them to set the injured man on it. Since both feet had been hurt, he stooped to remove his other boot. Once he'd set it aside, he looked up at the other soldiers, intending to tell them to get out.

"Hey, your eyes." The one with the cut up feet said it, staring at Liam's icy blue, almond shaped eyes. The other four snapped their attention to him.

He knew he had unusual eyes. In his social circles, people noticed and considered him exotic for them, and thus more desirable. Before he met Elena, he'd played on it to get what he wanted, often. These men staring at him, however, pushed outside his comfort zone. "Yes, they're unusual," he said curtly. "Privacy, please."

No one moved. "Are you a faith healer?" Despite the fact none of these men wore any rank insignia, he guessed this must be the higher one.

Liam snorted. "No." He pointed to the silver bar on his uniform shirt collar. He'd been given the Lieutenant rank to make his life smoother in the camp, though he hadn't actually been inducted into the Army. The General who'd handed him the insignia had gotten short with him when he'd insisted upon making that clear. "I believe I gave an order, gentlemen."

"Then what can you do? Is it anything like turning into a scad of itty bitty dragons?"

Two things annoyed Liam right now: these men refused to obey him, and he hated explaining this. A surge of raw, icy panic surged in his gut, eclipsing both things. "What? Where did you see dragons?" His hand shook as he reached up to check the man's temperature. His skin felt no warmer or cooler than anyone else's, which meant he had no easy excuse to discount anything he said.

"His name's Bobby. He said we shouldn't talk about him, but if you're one of them, it probably doesn't matter as much. Right?" The other four nodded slowly as the injured man spoke.

Liam paled. 'Bobby' could only be Mitchell, the one responsible for all that footage he saw of that apocalypse-level chaos in Salt Lake City. Privek called him dangerous, and the footage backed him up. On top of that, Mitchell had most likely been behind Elena's abduction. He tried not to gulp too hard. "Did he do this to your feet?"

"No." The injured man raised an eyebrow and snorted. "He rescued us. Him and the vampire one."

"Stephen," one of the others supplied. "We'd still be POWs getting tortured for information if they didn't show up."

Liam had no idea what to do with that information. Stephen the vampire must be Cant. The report said he might have drank blood from one of the nurses, but she couldn't really remember. By all accounts, Cant might be worse than Mitchell. Liam had been warned to watch out for them trying to lure him into a life of crime, or something along those lines. "Oh. I'm...glad to hear that. I, ah, do something like faith healing, but without the faith part."

He healed the man's feet and sent the soldiers on their way. "I need a break," he told his assistant.

She handed him another towel. "You just started an hour ago."

"Yeah," he snapped, "and now I need a break." He wiped off his feet and pulled his socks and boots back on. "I'll be back in a few minutes. Just need some air." Fleeing the tent, he sucked in a lungful of dry, warm air and let the morning sun bake him for a few minutes.

The monsters in the images he'd seen wouldn't have rescued soldiers. They would've killed everyone and moved on. More importantly, he had no idea why those two would come all the way here to kill people. They could go berserk in the States without the bother of traveling. He wondered if they'd come here to kill or abduct someone specific and rescued those soldiers by accident.

Maybe he should find them. Men able to empathize with imprisoned soldiers might listen to reason and be persuaded to release Elena. If he played his cards right, he could even talk them into working for Privek. As much as he hated the situation that agent had put him into, Privek clearly wanted the best outcome for all of them. Besides, they probably wouldn't attack him because of their common parent.

Hurrying through the camp, he peered around tents and vehicles until he spotted Mitchell with another man, both wearing desert camouflage. They sat on rocks at the perimeter, chatting. Cant had to be the second man. He'd been told the man had a sensitivity to sunlight, and he wore too much clothing for the heat. Cant reached over and shoved Mitchell playfully in the arm, Mitchell laughed and shook his head. They seemed so normal.

He took one step toward them, then froze. What if there was a reason—a very good reason—why he shouldn't walk over there and introduce himself? They wore uniforms and appeared to belong, making him wonder why. His hand found the bar on his own collar and he rubbed it between a finger and thumb.

Privek could be using them, or working his own angle for converting them. If he walked over there and said the wrong thing, he could ruin a lot of work. It would be easy to get huffy with Elena on the line, and his head full of people having their arms ripped off by their werewolf buddy. No, he needed to stay away from them. Elena needed him to do what he promised he'd do.

He took one last look before turning away and hoping his choice meant Elena would be back in his arms soon.

CHAPTER 7

"And they're sure these guys got some of our guys?"

Stephen snorted. "Only as sure as they were of that weapons cache."

Frowning, Bobby looked down at the asphalt under his boots. Airstrikes had smashed the buildings on either side of it to rubble, yet left the road intact. Though only about half of it had been demolished, the entire town had been abandoned, and Klein said a Taliban unit had moved in. According to him, they had 'reason to believe' at least three American soldiers could be found imprisoned here. Three men maybe held someplace wasn't enough to justify a conventional rescue operation.

"I reckon some scouting's in order, then."

"I agree. I'll wait overhead." Stephen went up without further discussion, leaving Bobby alone in the dark.

"Yeah," he muttered. Stephen's presence had more to do now with giving Bobby someone to talk to and a second brain to chew on things than anything else. Otherwise, the vampire had, more or less, become excess baggage and they both knew it. Bobby let the dragons peel away, sending them in to check out the town. It spread out, darting around and through the rubble, then into the intact buildings.

By the time they finished, they'd found three buildings they couldn't get into without Bobby specifically directing them. The swarm came back together and he set them on the task of breaking into the first one. Its appearance and size suggested a warehouse. Dragons found their way in through one of his favorite access points, an air vent. The place had been set up as an ambush, with tripwires, explosives, even simple stakes and stairs rigged to collapse.

At first, he couldn't understand why they thought anyone would fall for this, or why they'd enter it at all. Then he found the odd little devices clipped to the power lines. Aside from the surprise of finding power out here, he had no idea what to make of the devices. Several dragons fell on the boxes to figure out what they were.

The devices had no buttons or dials, switches or levers. The cord appeared to be a standard three-prong power cable, with no extra wires. It had no antennas, and emitted no sounds or signals he could pick up. They did give off heat, like any other electronic gadget. It seemed to be their sole purpose, which made no sense to him. In a place already hotter'n heckbiscuits this time of year, they had a series of tiny space heaters.

His dragons poked and prodded at the things until they noticed the devices emitted not heat, but a *specific temperature*. The surrounding air matched what the dragons knew to be his own natural body temperature. It took him another minute to think of a reason anyone might want that.

These things had to be intended to fool detection methods that searched for body heat. For a moment, he admired the ingenuity of whoever came up with them. If a normal military unit came in to rescue those men, they'd be lured to a building full of death. Riding on the heels of this realization, seething rage threatened to overpower him. The swarm wanted to find whoever created these death traps and rip them apart from the inside out.

The second building proved to be empty. When he breached the third building, he figured he'd find people, and meant to scout it and return to Stephen to plan. In the first room they found, the dragons saw men sitting around a table, playing cards and speaking some kind of Arabic-type language. They bore a strong resemblance to the men in that cave system. Before he realized he needed to restrain them, the dragons poured out and attacked, flooding the room and diving into the throats of the surprised men.

Bobby watched the men thrash and gurgle, watched them claw at their throats and chests. They exploded, dragons bursting out in enough places to rip their chests and backs and bellies apart. In seconds, his swarm reduced four men to shredded meat and sprayed blood and gore everywhere. Dragon fire sparked all around as they cleaned each other off, and he pulled them in to re-form and survey their handiwork with his own eyes.

Fresh meat, blood, bile: they mixed together in a horrible stench. They had died so fast, with so much awful violence. He would never have to worry about dying like that. What did that mean? Anything at all? He covered his mouth and swallowed bile. Turning on his heel, he slipped and grabbed the bloody doorknob to steady himself.

He shut the door behind himself and sagged against it, breathing in the dirt and sweat and dust of the hallway. No matter how many times he wiped his hand on his pants, it refused to feel clean, and he swiped his hat off to wipe his sleeve across his brow. He'd come here to scout, not to slaughter.

Somewhere else in the hallway, a door opened and shut. It goaded him to stagger away from the door and move. His boots clomped on the thin, industrial carpet and he used the wall for support. As he passed it, a door opened, smacking into his side. The man behind it stared, wide-eyed, then he raised his assault rifle and pointed it at Bobby's chest. He said something.

The dragons yearned to be freed. Bobby clamped them down and raised his hands. "I only speak English," he informed the man, which earned him a rough nudge in the arm with the gun.

"Go," the man said with a thick accent.

Bobby let himself be shoved along, too numb and distracted to resist. As he went, the guy shoved the gun barrel into his back on one side or the other at random intervals, and it got so annoying that Bobby recovered his wits. He could get away at any moment, but this guy seemed to have a destination in mind, and it could turn out to be where the prisoners were kept. That would make everything faster and simpler.

They went down three flights of metal stairs, two more than necessary to reach the ground. Finally, they passed through a door and down another hallway. Bobby got shoved into an empty room with a bare earth floor and walls. The door clanged shut and his host jangled keys, then he said something that sounded like a sarcastic welcome and walked away. Though the dragons wanted to stream out the window with the bars across it to destroy that man, Bobby wanted to wait and learn more first.

"Hey," he called out. Moving over to the door, he grabbed the bars and stood on his toes. He managed to get high enough to peer out, doing it for the sake of appearances. "Hey, is anybody out there?"

"Yeah," a male voice croaked. "Save your strength." He had a Bronx accent, and sounded tired and defeated. "They'll be down for you soon enough."

"What'd they do to you?" He hated to ask and would have preferred never to know. Someone in his position would ask. Besides, better to hear about it before seeing it.

"Doesn't matter. Not getting out of here no matter what."

Bobby took a deep breath and forced the dragons to stay put. "Anybody else down here?"

"Yeah. You make eight. If Turtle's still alive."

"I'm here," a voice called out, reedy and in obvious and extreme pain. "Sort of."

Great, just great. Bobby leaned his forehead against the door, trying to cool the rage in the dragons. His own anger worked against him. Before he went on another murdering spree, though, he wanted to be able to say they'd deserved it beyond a shadow of a doubt. "Why ain't they just killed ya?"

The first voice huffed out what might have been a laugh if he had more energy for it. "I think these sonsabitches just like torturing us. They ask questions, but it doesn't matter what we answer. Might as well be asking what time it is for all they seem to care about the answers. Face facts, kid, you're in for a long, slow, painful wait for the day when they finally decide to let you die."

"Butler got out." This voice came from a cell deeper down the hallway, and had a mild East LA accent.

"Butler killed himself," the first guy snorted.

"How long you guys been down here?"

"Who the fuck knows." The first guy coughed, and it sounded wet and unpleasant. "Shit, I'm spitting blood again."

Now, he'd heard enough. The swarm burst violently out and poured through the window. Dragons attacked the other doors, pulling, pushing, burning, and scraping. They ripped apart hinges and handles, and the doors fell into the hallway with clangs that had to echo up the stairs. Men would come, soon, to investigate the noise. The swarm flowed to the only exit—the stairs he'd been brought down—to ravage whoever came down. He had enough presence of mind to send five dragons to get Stephen.

Frothing, burning rage carried the dragons through the entire building, spreading out to make sure no one escaped. They churned through every human in the building, except those seven prisoners, and Bobby let them do it without reservation. Whatever had happened to those men down there, it had been gratuitous and cruel and unnecessary. What happened to Riker and his men almost seemed reasonable and justifiable in comparison.

When Bobby re-formed in the middle of the worst of it on the ground floor, he could hear Stephen outside the door, probably there to get better reception for his earpiece.

"Cant and Mitchell reporting in. There are seven wounded men here. The building has been cleared. So far as we can tell, there's no one else in this town. None of these men can walk on their own, so we need on-site evac and it'd be best if you send at least one medic to bundle them up for travel...I didn't get names. Some of them can't talk in their current condition, and the ones that can aren't in good shape. It's questionable whether they'll all actually survive until you can get someone here...You maybe want to inform the evac people that the site is—" He coughed. "They should be prepared for carnage."

Bobby stared at his handiwork, empty inside. 'Carnage', Stephen called it. This time, he had no urge to throw up and no idea what that meant. Maybe he'd been born for this, designed by those scientists to be an unstoppable killing machine. Up until this trip, he'd thought of the dragons as scouts, not machines of death. Now he knew better.

"We'll do what we can," Stephen said, still talking to Klein, "but we aren't medics and have no idea what will make things worse. In fact, it might be in our bests interests to leave before anyone gets here. They're in the basement." He stepped back inside. Bobby heard more than saw him. "Are you okay?"

Yeah, he was all full of peaches and sunshine. Bobby's expression went sour as he noticed his stomach growling. At a time like this, surrounded by bodies destroyed by his dragons, he was hungry. "No."

"Maybe you should get some air." Stephen headed for the stairs. "I'm going to do what I can to make sure these guys last until help gets here, but then we should go."

He could turn his back on all of this and put it behind him. No one expected him to do more than he already had, not even Stephen. He rubbed his face with both hands and heard his daddy's voice in his head, telling him to stop being a weak, lazy lump. Fleeing now would be just that: fleeing. Momma didn't raise a coward, and he could face this.

He stepped over a charred pile of shredded meat and pulled a protein bar out of his pocket. "I want to see them."

"Didn't you see them already?"

"No, we weren't looking. Kinda focused on bad guys."

Stephen glanced over as they took the stairs down together, his eyes flicking from food to face. He said nothing, though. They reached the bottom and the vampire pointed at one door. "That one's the worst."

Nodding his understanding, Bobby stopped before he could see inside any of the doors and let Stephen go ahead. Despite his certainty upstairs, he hesitated now. The vampire continued on and disappeared into one of the cells, unruffled by any of this. It seemed that he had no problem stomaching anything he hadn't caused himself.

Bobby frowned at the ground, trying to figure out what bothered him more about the men down here than what he'd done upstairs. He didn't do any of this. He couldn't have prevented it. He hadn't failed to act. Someone did, someone could have, someone had, but not him. What, then, was he afraid of? He stood there, trying to figure it out and listened to Stephen talking to one of the men.

"They're on their way. No idea how long it will take. I think you're in decent enough condition I could move you, but I'm not sure it's wise."

"It'll probably hurt a lot." The other voice was that Bronx guy. "Then the medics will come and do more. Yeah, maybe I should just stay put. How's Turtle?"

"Turtle's screwed, that's how he is." Turtle sounded worse now, as if his condition had deteriorated since Bobby last heard him. His breaths came out ragged and labored, and every word cost him something to force out. "Would you guys tell my mom I'm sorry I didn't listen to her when she begged me not to join?"

"Tell her yourself," Bronx called back.

Turtle made a noise that could have been a strained laugh or a stifled sob. "Not likely."

Either Stephen or Bronx muttered something too low to be understood, then the vampire paced out of that first room. He paused in the hallway and looked over Bobby questioningly. He opened his mouth to say something, but stopped and closed it, then shook his head with a sigh and went for the next room.

Whatever his intention with that, the gesture made Bobby's feet take him to the first room, where he looked in and saw a cell no different from the one he'd been tossed into. Bronx wore a pair of khaki pants ripped off at the knees and nothing else. He sat with his back against the far wall, covered in dried blood and dirt. His left foot—Bobby knew was no other word for it than 'mangled'. If he had to guess how it'd been done, he'd say someone shoved it into a meat grinder, then let it 'heal' that way. Strangely shaped burn marks and acid scars covered his chest. They chopped three fingers off his right hand and split the big toe on his right foot in half. Bobby's brain refused to figure out what had happened to the man's right knee, but it looked wrong.

That didn't even qualify as 'the worst'. "Hey," he said to Bronx, because the man noticed him there. "I'm, uh, the guy what was in that cell." The dragons wanted to burst out and kill those men all over again. And again and again, until nothing remained but pulpy piles of sludge.

"You busted us out?"

Now, he wanted to throw up. Swallowing bile back down, he gave a vague little nod of his head with a shrug of his shoulders. "Yeah, with Stephen. It was kinda an unplanned jailbreak kinda thing. I weren't rightly expecting what I done found here."

Bronx's mouth lifted in a strained, lopsided smile. "Thanks, man. I dunno how you did it, but you did."

Looking down at the floor, Bobby scuffed a boot and tried not to show what he actually felt. The damage done to this guy's body repulsed him, and he hated himself for it. Pity filled him for what he'd go through starting tomorrow, and he hated himself for that, too. Worse, he couldn't figure out what to say. Everything that came to mind seemed stupid or pointless. "Wish I'd'a been here six months ago."

"You and me both." Bronx coughed. It might have been a laugh. "I figure I'll be in a wheelchair when I get home, but hey, at least I won't be here or dead, right?"

"Yeah, that's something."

"It's okay, man, I know it's hard to look at. I been living with it for a while and I don't want to look, either."

"There anything I can get you?"

Someone else called out, "You got a girl in your pocket?"

Bobby got a ghost of a smile. "Nah, sorry. If it makes you feel any better, though, I ain't got laid in a while, neither." He cringed, not sure if that was an okay thing to joke about, not sure if it even came off as one.

Bronx cough-chuckled. "Big damn hero like you doesn't have 'em lined up around the corner? Must be doing something wrong." Bobby also heard a few pain-spiced sounds of amusement from the other rooms.

"Yeah, I reckon so. Guess I gotta brag more or something. Any of you got girls back home already?" Was this helping? Talking to them about stupid crap—did that help, or make things worse? He had no clue, but at least, he supposed, he had them thinking about something besides their own misery.

"I got a wife," a new voice said, strained and kind of soft. "She was pregnant when I left. I have a little girl I've never met. I guess I'll get to spend some quality time with my girls now."

"I had a girlfriend," Hispanic said, and he sighed. "I expect she's long gone by now."

"I got a girl back home, but she's..." Bobby paused and breathed, trying to get the anger to drain down. None of that was for Lily, he only had frustration about her. I don't think it's gonna work out anyway."

"Oh, come on," Bronx cajoled. "What'd she do? Bite your dick? Sleep around? Get pissy about you joining up?" A few of the others echoed his interest, trying to get Bobby to open up and tell them what happened.

It made no sense to him. Why did they want to hear about his love life? All that seemed stupid and petty compared to what they'd lived with for the past few months and would deal with for the rest of their lives. Enough of them piped up and urged him, though, that he told them. "She was married right outta high school, the guy was some kinda bigger damn hero than me. He come over here in the Army, I think, got himself killed a few years ago. She's got his little boy, and she's still in love with him. Last time I saw her, she called me by his name. Ring ain't there, but it is, you know? Private First Class Thatcher, might as well be Saint Sebastian for her."

"Thatcher?" Hispanic asked. "The wife is a hot brunette with these kinda funny blue eyes?"

Bobby blinked a few times. Bronx beat him to answering. "From the look on his face, I'd say that's a 'yeah'."

"Huh, small goddamned world. Thatcher was in my unit when I first got here. We were both green as shit. He had a picture of her he kept in his helmet. Didn't even know the baby was going to be a boy. Good guy. He got off easy. Pushed me out of the way and took the hit that shoulda taken me out. No idea why. If I had a girl like that back home, I wouldn't have done that."

Now he knew how the guy died, and it made things worse. He was a real hero, the kind Bobby wasn't and would never be. "Thanks, I feel tons better now," he grumbled. Rubbing his face with a hand, he sighed heavily and tried not to think about her. It didn't work.

Bronx cough-chuckled again. "I think you done a little better than saving one guy."

"I guess that depends on how you look at it." Bobby glanced at Bronx and shook his head. "Pretty sure she ain't taking me back after I left like how I did."

Several of them laughed at him, and he decided they'd more than earned the right to do it. It all faded away into coughing and then quiet until he could hear Stephen murmuring to Turtle in that second room.

Bobby had a thought to try another subject to keep them entertained. When he opened his mouth, Stephen's voice rang out.

"I'd really appreciate if you guys could convince Turtle he wants to live."

The request forced Bobby to move, bring him to the doorway where Stephen sat with his back against the wall, unhappy and exasperated. The other guy's body had been broken in so many ways Bobby couldn't even comprehend what they did to him to make it happen, or how he'd managed to survive this long. A long list of thing that guy could never hope to do again filled his head, starting with 'walking' and rolling through everything imaginable that would be fun. In his opinion, the man ought to be allowed to die if he wanted to.

"Turtle," Bronx called out, "you still got your mind. Whatever they did to your body, they never took away what's in your head."

Whatever happened to a man's body, it didn't have to happen to his head. Bobby stood there and thought about that, wondering if it rightly applied to him. Was he still the same guy as before? No, not at all. A month and a half ago, he had a decent job and didn't cause any— Except for how he went over and punched Mr. Peterson in the face for what he did to Momma. If he had the dragons then, would he have killed the man? Did he blame the dragons for his own anger? If all they did was make it more obvious and easier to give in to, what did that really mean?

Vaguely, he heard Turtle respond. "Like none of us has nightmares every night, like any of us is ever going to be okay. I'm not—I'm not strong enough for this."

Bobby realized he'd fallen into staring, and that his mind had started to really see and comprehend the horrific state of the man's body. Not wanting to live with that, he forced himself to refocus on Stephen. The vampire wanted to avoid another mercy killing. No matter how little it bothered him to snap the neck of someone who wanted to kill him back, the idea of sucking out Turtle's life bothered him. Even if all three of them could see, plain as day, that it would be right thing to do.

He opened his mouth for Stephen's sake, not Turtle's. "I ain't rightly sure what comes after. I been raised to think it's Heaven, that we all get to see folks we lost and be happy all the time and all that. More I see and do, though, more I wonder if'n that's true. There's lots of things that're just as likely as what the preacher done told me, including nothing. I know you done suffered a lot, and I don't think nobody'd really blame you for wanting that to end.

"Thing is, what if there's a girl waiting to meet you, maybe in the hospital or something, or a doctor what needs to see what happened to you to make some kinda leap in logic or something to make a new kinda thing for a kid what needs help? What if you're stronger than you think and it ain't a nightmare ahead of you?"

He felt cheap and slimy for trying to talk Turtle into living. The guy was crippled, wouldn't have a real life ever again, and Bobby plain didn't have to ever consider the prospect of facing that. If he got mangled up like that, he'd go swarm and re-form and everything would be put back. He had no right to try to guilt someone else into living with something he'd never have to.

Turtle didn't answer. Stephen looked up at Bobby in surprise. It was in his expression; he could tell Bobby only said all that to try to spare him, and couldn't decide how to feel about that. The vampire looked back at Turtle and sighed heavily. "It's your life, your choice."

Unwilling to watch the guy choose, Bobby walked away and peered into the next door. He paused and nodded to the guy there, then moved on to the next one and continued until he reached the last one. Most of them had similar problems as Bronx. One of them lay unconscious, breathing with a wet raspy sound to it. He might never wake up.

"Somebody tell my mom this isn't her fault," Turtle rasped.

Bronx answered, voice shaky, "Yeah, I will. Rest well, buddy."

A gasp came from Turtle's room, then a little moan with no pain in it. "Thank you," he whispered.

Bobby hurried for the stairs to get away from that. He and Stephen needed to get the heckbiscuits out of here and move on to the next mission. That one would be simpler, and they'd handle it and move on, and it would only take a few more until Privek would let them in. They'd find Jasmine and free her and go home.

Outside the door, he leaned against the wall and closed his eyes, wishing he could unsee everything inside. The dragons still wanted to destroy people, or was that him? Either way, he only held them back because they'd already killed everyone here.

Stephen stormed out a few minutes later, throwing the door open hard enough to tear it off the hinges and send it flying several feet away. He didn't want to talk. It seemed to Bobby that he needed a trenchcoat billowing out around him to go with that angry swagger. The vampire took to the air and Bobby followed him as dragons, keeping them all out of arm's reach, just in case. For both their sakes.

CHAPTER 8

The flight to the next target lasted long enough for Bobby to get frustrated by his failure to collect his thoughts into true coherence. He wanted to specifically not think about what had happened at that warehouse. More than that, he needed to exact revenge for it, yet all those responsible had already been killed. That minor detail irritated him, and he flicked it aside.

Of course, all these people, the ones who lived here and thought the same way and looked the same and followed the same religion should be held responsible. They hadn't prevented it, they hadn't stopped it, they hadn't condemned it. The only way to save more lives, the lives that mattered, would be to kill them all. None of them deserved to live, and all of them had to die to protect Jasmine and Liam and Paul and the rest.

They descended on an armed compound. Neither Bobby nor Stephen cared about double-checking on the mission. Not this time. Both had frustration and anger to vent, and nothing could stop them. Since all of these people bore guilt, Bobby wasted no time with scouting.

Stephen started on one side, and Bobby went from the other. They moved through it and slaughtered everyone, meeting in the middle. Bobby re-formed in time to watch the dragons that made up his hands burst out through the chests of three different men, all of them screaming as they fell to the ground.

It didn't bother him. These men had tortured Bronx and Turtle and Riker by proxy. Given the chance, they'd do the same thing to someone else. The fact they found no American soldiers here meant only that they hadn't managed to capture any for whatever reason, or the ones they captured were already dead and the bodies disposed of. These people had blood on their hands, he knew it.

Stephen pushed his way out of the small room off to the side, wiping blood off his chin with one hand while he tucked his shirt into his pants with the other. His expression mirrored how Bobby felt as he stood there, finishing off a chicken leg he picked up off a table: pleased, sated, and righteous. He tossed the bone over his shoulder and stepped over bodies to join the vampire.

This place had also sated and pleased the dragons. They'd stopped pressing to break free, stopped pushing him to do something. He felt pretty good, too. They'd done something important, something worth doing. This scum had to be wiped off the face of the Earth, and he and Stephen were just the right tools for that job. Admittedly, he didn't need Stephen all that much. For just cleansing this plague, he could handle that on his own.

They landed inside the small forward base nearest to where they'd been busy tonight. "Cant and Mitchell reporting in," Stephen told his earpiece. "Mission complete, we're stopping for tonight. I'll call back in before dusk again." They strode through the base together, Bobby having no idea of their destination. "Understood." Stephen pulled the earpiece out again. "The unconscious guy didn't survive being loaded for transport. The rest are either on the table or otherwise stable. So, five made it."

Bobby nodded and tried to ignore the flashes of fresh memory.

"Maybe we oughta split up. Get more done at once."

Stephen stopped and put a hand out to grab Bobby's arm, making him stop, too. "What are you talking about? We're not here to get as much done as possible, we're here to get Privek to trust us. Bobby, this isn't about killing people, this is about getting closer to finding the others. Did you forget that already?"

Scowling, Bobby looked away. "I didn't forget nothing."

The vampire pulled his hand away and crossed his arms, also looking off at nothing in particular. "We were going to stick together for a reason. After what happened last night, I don't think..." He sighed and shifted uncomfortably. "You didn't want to deal with those soldiers. Someone had to. What would you do if you wound up in that situation again?"

He knew the vampire was right. It changed nothing. "I ain't helpless or nothing."

"I'm not your dad." Stephen snorted. "If you want to go it alone, it's not like I can stop you. But, you don't have one of these," he held up the earpiece he used to contact Klein, "and I'm not giving you this one, because I need it, too." Before Bobby considered swiping it, Stephen tucked the device back into his pocket. "I'm going to get some sleep. Which is your cue to eat. See you later."

Annoyed, Bobby shrugged it off and gave Stephen a curt, unenthusiastic nod. His stomach growled with the mention of food, so he sniffed the air and headed for the mess tent in a sulk. He didn't need Stephen, not to do this stuff. The vampire was smarter than him, he knew that. Stephen didn't know everything, and these missions had nothing to do with brains. No one could stop him, and he had no need for someone to watch his back.

Brooding at his food tray, he shoveled food into his mouth without tasting it, a tactic that served him well out here. Whether Stephen wanted to admit it or not, this mission only needed killing, and he now had the best way ever conceived to do that. His entire body was made of hundreds of little assassins. Stephen didn't think he could handle himself on his own. No one ever did. He could, and he would.

Of course, that did nothing to dispel the ghost of Saint Sebastian lingering at his back. Bobby had no idea how the guy's voice sounded, but he could hear it anyway, telling him how he didn't stand a chance, how Lily could see right through him. Sebastian would always be the better man, because he'd sacrificed everything to be a hero.

Bobby sacrificed nothing. He could kill everyone in the country—no, everyone in the world—without suffering so much as a paper cut. Sebastian had been a normal guy, rising above his human limitations. Bobby had no limitations to rise above.

Before now, he hadn't dwelt on how thoroughly unstoppable he'd become. The suits stopped him by catching him off guard, in his human costume. What would happen if someone chopped his head off while he was drugged and couldn't go swarm? That was an experiment he'd rather not try. Like Stephen, he preferred to just not know the extent of his nigh-immortality. But, out here, no one had that drug. The sooner he killed all these terrorists, the sooner Privek would declare the mission complete. He ought to get on with it.

Resolved to end this war on his own, he crammed the rest of his meal into his mouth and hurried out of there. He didn't know where exactly to go, but how hard could it be to find people that wanted to kill American soldiers when he looked like one? Not hard at all. At the edge of the camp, he broke into the swarm and flew up and away. So far, all the missions took them to the north part of the country, so he went that way.

Landing just outside a small town an hour or so later, he walked boldly down the road. A stone wall about five feet high all the way around the low, squat buildings all squished together in a clump. Four men loitered with assault rifles in front of the wooden gate, watching and pointing at Bobby as he got close. Considering nothing else had probably happened near them in a while, he took no offense at the pointing.

Going by looks alone, these men needed killing. They looked the same as those other men, the ones he knew deserved the unpleasant deaths he gave them. But he couldn't be completely sure everyone here needed that kind of judgment passed on them, and thought he ought to give them a chance before meting it out.

Approaching the four men, he held up his hands and let them take a good look. He stopped twenty feet away and turned around to prove he had no weapons. Their actions would decide how this went, not his.

Two pointed their guns at Bobby, one held his more casually, and the fourth rested his against his shoulder, looking unconcerned with this foreigner on his turf. He was the biggest, taller than Bobby and more muscular, and stood with his feet apart enough to be intimidating with his confidence. Intimidating to someone actually worried about death or debilitating injury, anyway. Bobby gave the guy some respect for show.

"Hi there," he called out. "Don't s'pose any of ya speak English?"

Confident Man nodded. "Some. What you want, American?"

Bobby suddenly realized he needed a story. It had to be something where they'd feel free to treat him however they wanted, instead of how he wanted them to based upon a gun to their heads. "I got separated from my unit, and kinda need to use a phone or something. If'n you can spare it, a drink of water'd be appreciated, too."

Confident Man turned enough to speak to the others, using another language, and chuckling at some grand joke. Casual Rifle Guy grinned and replied, jerking his chin to indicate Bobby. Confident Man eyed Bobby up like a predator checking out potential food. "Come, phone."

Anyone else would have been six kinds of stupid to follow that man. Someone genuinely in the situation he pretended to would be better off wandering around in hopes of bumping into Americans. Bobby, though, smiled. "Thank you kindly." He ambled after the man, acting like a stupid hick. Stephen would probably tell him that he came to the role naturally, and he'd be right.

As expected, Casual Rifle Guy tried to use the butt of his rifle to hit Bobby in the back of the head. Instead of the impact the guy hoped for, Bobby burst into dragons and let them run wild. It took them half an hour to spread through the town and kill all the men. Women and children, he left alone. Without pausing to examine his handiwork in human shape, he put the town behind him and moved on.

That term, 'human shape', covered it. He wasn't human, he had a shape that appeared human. In reality, he was a great big bunch of dragons all linked together. His life up until he discovered that had been pretend, or maybe learning how to blend in. Considering it that way, he didn't deserve to be considered a murderer. Instead, he ought to be thought of as a janitor. They should to thank him, even, for cleaning up their stupid messes. They weren't even worth getting fussed up over, anyway. Anything that could die so easily couldn't have much value.

He let the landscape go by under the swarm, only stopping when he saw another town. This time, as soon as he saw the men who looked exactly like those other ones, he let the swarm go without bothering to pause and check them out. Because they didn't matter to him, he let the dragons kill whoever they wanted without paying attention. Instead, he floated in the middle of the bloodbath, trying to figure himself out.

If he was a big pile of dragons, what *was* the 'Bobby' part of him, this overall mind? He remembered seeing a TV show once where a bunch of little things that were dumb individually got smart when they all came together. That seemed to kind of fit, though he couldn't imagine how it must work. Loosed from a physical shell, it didn't make any sense that his consciousness actually came from his brain, though when he tried to move the part that he knew to specifically be 'Bobby', nothing happened. He was as chained to the dragons as they were to him.

The thought kept him busy until the dragons swarmed together again, burning the blood off of each others' tiny bodies. Letting them do what they wanted to these people took no effort on his part, and even felt good, like relaxing a muscle he hadn't noticed was tense.

In the next town, the dragons went through and killed everyone, then he found an empty bed in a room with no bodies or gore and lay down to grab himself some rest. He fell asleep easily. When he woke, vague impressions of unpleasant dreams sat on his shoulders. Standing and stretching brushed them away.

The sun set while he rummaged through the kitchen. He found crackers, raw vegetables that tasted fine, and some pastes and sauces he liked. One tub in the fridge had some chicken with lentils he devoured with gusto.

"Bobby, are you still here?" Stephen's voice drifted through the window from the street below.

How did the vampire find him? He scratched his cheek and figured that ignoring Stephen would be childish. Instead of shouting out the window, he went dragon and poured out of the house, re-forming on the street a few feet away from Stephen. "Yeah, I'm here." The stench of death—raw and rotting meat, blood, urine, feces, bile—hung heavy here, and flies buzzed everywhere.

Stephen held an arm up to shield his nose. "I see you've been busy."

"Ain't no sense in waiting."

The vampire pulled his arm down and rested both hands on his hips. "No? Am I slowing you down by giving a shot at trying to determine if people we kill actually need to be killed or not?"

This sounded like the start of a lecture. Bobby's eyes narrowed and he scowled. "If'n you got something to say, then say it."

Instead of answering, Stephen pointed. Bobby's eyes followed the line of the gloved finger until he saw it. A little boy lay surrounded by his own gore, dead eyes staring up at the sky. Next to him was a woman that might be his mother, also dead. She held an infant in her arms, also ripped apart. The handiwork was obviously his own; no one else came and did this while he slept, but he didn't remember doing it. He hadn't been paying attention while the dragons exercised their freedom.

Bobby turned away from that horror and found himself looking at another two young children, faces twisted in terror. He'd casually murdered children whose only possible crime was being born here instead of someplace else. By not caring enough to keep track of the dragons, by feeding their blind rage, he killed these kids, that mother, that baby. He could live with killing grown men who took up arms to fight. Little kids, though...

Bending over, he put his hands on his knees and threw up into the street. Everything he ate came back up, most of it still recognizable. Stephen stood by in silence, only moving a foot to stay clear of the new mess. When he had nothing left inside, Bobby suffered through a few dry heaves, then took a drink from the canteen Stephen offered him and spat it out.

"I thought maybe you'd had a psychotic break." Stephen took the canteen back and tucked it away in a pocket.

"What did I do," Bobby breathed, eyes wide and staring. "What did I do?"

"That's an excellent question. Offhand, it looks like you decided to pass judgment on a few thousand people, if you count the ones in the other two places you went through." Stephen's voice held no emotion, only detached curiosity. "Which is interesting, since you're so disturbed by my drinking blood, something I am forced to do to continue living and which does not require the death of my victim. As I recall, it also disturbed you when I discovered how much I enjoy killing someone when I do it."

Bobby stumbled back a few steps, tripped over something, and landed on his backside in congealed blood mixed with other things. His mouth moved, but no sound came out. He killed these kids and that baby, and others like them. What was he doing when the dragons forced their way into these little mouths? Pondering his existence? Thinking. When he should have been acting, when he should have been in control, he'd been thinking about life, about his invincibility, about his superiority.

Stepping gingerly to Bobby's side, Stephen offered him a hand. "We need to get you out of here, Bobby. I thought I was the one that would have trouble with all this, but it's you."

"What did I do?" Bobby stared at Stephen's hand, not sure what to do with it, not sure if he deserved it.

"Only you can answer that question." Stephen reached down and took Bobby's hand, pulling him to his feet. "Let's go ponder it someplace else. The ambiance here hasn't been improved by adding your breakfast to it."

Afraid to let the dragons out, Bobby stood there, his mind gone blank. Stephen solved the problem by hefting him in a fireman's carry and flying upwards. Slung there like a sack of potatoes, Bobby chased circles in his head. Those people died because he'd failed to prevent the dragons from killing them. He'd spent his time worrying about himself and ignoring the rest of the world, and those people all paid the price for it.

Stephen flew for a while in the darkness, then touched down in a spot with nothing around for miles. He dumped Bobby into a pile of wild grass where he got an unobstructed view of the star-filled sky. No light pollution spoiled the view, and he stared up at the impossibly full, moonless night.

All those millions of sparkly dots burned with heat so intense his dragons wouldn't withstand it. They stared down at him, not giving a crap about his problems or confusions or wonderings. Once upon a time, he might have prayed to God for forgiveness, but had had no idea if that would help now. It didn't feel like that mattered much.

Several minutes later, he said, "The dragons, they're me and I'm them." He left it there for a bit, feeling small and insignificant compared to the sky. A few minutes later, he he opened his mouth again, not sure what would tumble out of it. "I keep thinking of them as something else, but they're me. I'm all little bitty parts jammed together into one bigger piece. What they want, it's what I want. They did all that while I wasn't paying attention, only I was, because they're me. I knew what they were doing."

"They controlled you instead of you controlling them," Stephen murmured into the darkness.

"Yeah. And no. And yeah." Nothing had changed since he killed those two suits, other than efficiency. Then, he'd been surprised they could do such a thing at all. Now...he didn't want to think about it something this confusing and disturbing. "I gotta get outta here, afore I ain't nothing left worth having."

For a few minutes, Stephen said nothing. He stood nearby, also staring up at the sky with his hands in his pockets. "Agreed. Let's get moving. If we're lucky, we can get a fair distance before anyone notices we've gone."

Bobby let the dragons peel off, ready to carry his own weight again, at least for traveling. It would be unfair to expect Stephen to haul him any further. Not that fair had a seat at his table right now, but if he wanted to take control back, he had to start someplace. "What about Privek?"

"Screw Privek. None of those eleven would want you to sacrifice your sanity, to become a monster just to get them free."

Uncertain how to take that, Bobby nodded before his head dispersed into dragons and had the swarm follow Stephen. They flew all night, pausing a few times to let Bobby eat, then went to ground for the day in some rural area Stephen thought might be in Turkey. As little as he liked them, Bobby choked down more of those stupid protein bars to keep his stomach under control.

"We're going to discuss what happened," Stephen said as he leaned against the rock of a shallow cave. The direction the mouth faced meant he could expect to be in the shade for most of the day.

"I ain't got nothing to say 'bout that." He sounded childish and knew it, and didn't care.

"Fine, then. You can listen." Stephen pulled his hat, sunglasses, and balaclava off, setting them aside and moving on to his gloves. He looked tired, which came as no surprise. Bobby suspected the vampire wouldn't take any crap from anyone right now. "To me, humans are basically overglorified cows. Walking, talking food. It's really difficult to actually care about them as people. Yet, I grew up thinking I was one of them. Sure, I always suspected I wasn't quite as normal as everyone around me was, but I was human as a child and had a family that cared about me. My parents are good people, so are my brother and sister. Pastor Chris is a good man.

"And yet, here I am, looking at people like that Elena chick and thinking 'food'." Stephen stared directly at Bobby, the weight of it so intense Bobby had to look away, down at the ground. "Since I've had a fair amount of time to think about this, it seems to me that is entirely because people are now food for me. At first, I bit my girlfriend during sex. Didn't even realize why I was doing it, I just did it. She didn't remember me doing it, and the sex was great. As women do, though, she got her period. She didn't like sex during that, said she felt too crappy. Which is fine, I could live for a week without sex. I still needed to eat, though.

"I didn't feel comfortable looking for a whore at the time, partly because of the stigma and partly because that would be cheating on Marie, and I wasn't sure where to go for that anyway. I also didn't feel like I could go to anyone I knew, because it was so crazy and demented. So I found a few homeless people and paid them ten bucks each to let me bite them. It was nothing like as great as sex and food together, but that was how I came to the understanding that drinking blood is an intimate thing, something inextricably linked with sex. Biting men bothered me because I'm not attracted to them.

"But, my point is that they're food. If I wanted to let that rule me, I could. There's no shame in slaughtering food animals, so long as you're actually eating them, and I've never managed to feel 'full', so I know I can drink more than one person dry at a time. Which, of course, means that I could pick people out and eat them and feel nothing, because they're just cows." He stopped there, still staring at him.

Bobby scowled at his feet, having a feeling he knew what the point might be. "But you ain't doing it," he mumbled to the dirt.

"No, I'm not. I could, and I already know what it feels like to do it — it's amazing and intense and I want that, badly. But I'm not doing it."

"And you think I'm an asshole for giving in."

Stephen arched an eyebrow up. "No, I think you allowed the dragons to become your scapegoat. Whatever they do, it's them, not you, and you can be disgusted by it without feeling responsible because they're not under your control. In reality, they're little pieces of you, Bobby, and you're completely responsible for everything they do. In the same way that my hunger for blood feels like a separate thing, a demon possessing me, if you will. I could blame it for whatever depraved things I do, but that's a lie, a bald lie. It's not some other entity, it's nothing more or less than my deepest, darkest desires, made more palpable for what I have to do to survive. This is about taking responsibility for what you are and can do. I understand you didn't quite realize what they're capable of, but now you do." He smirked. "If you keep letting them do it, *then* you're an asshole."

Bobby huffed out a very mild snort, but also nodded his understanding. They sat in silence for a few minutes while he chased his thoughts around to form them into coherence. "I ain't rightly sure what actually happens when I'm dragons. To me, I mean. I tried to see what I could do while they were- I let 'em go to just do whatever they wanted, and they flipped out at folks what look like those guys in the cave. In that first town, one tried to smack me upside the head with his rifle, and I let 'em loose, but we only done killed the men."

Thinking back, he replayed it, trying to figure out where things went wrong. But then, it had actually been before that. Maybe a lot before that. He never killed anyone until that day at Lily's house. Those two suits came in and the dragons surprised the heckbiscuits out of him by attacking.

They killed those two men. Because...because he was angry at the suits for what they did. At that point, though, they hadn't really done much. "I think...I think maybe I got lotta anger in me, and I just don't feel it so much because they do."

Several seconds passed before Stephen offered, "Maybe you should ask yourself why you have all that anger."

"Shoot, I dunno. I always been the scrawny kid, the one what got beat on, not the one what done the beating."

"You were bullied as a kid and you can't imagine why you might be angry as an adult?"

Bobby opened his mouth to respond, but realized he had no intelligent words to put there, so he shut it and looked off into the distance, making a little 'hm' noise. "I reckon maybe I gotta stew on this stuff."

"Probably wise." Stephen picked his hat back up and used it to mostly cover his face. "Don't forget I changed two months before you met me. Also, I had therapy when I was young."

CHAPTER 9

If anyone noticed them perched on the top of this cruise ship, Bobby would eat his boot. He sat next to Stephen in a t-shirt and boxers, working on a plate piled high with food. This was the best meal he'd had in a while —fried chicken, buttered corn on the cob, mashed potatoes slathered in gravy, thick biscuits, and a beer. His camouflage clothes lay in a rumpled pile nearby, where he'd shucked them to blend with the natives and enjoy the sunshine.

"This is the way to travel." He loosed a mighty burp. "They don't even ask nothing, cause ain't nobody should be on the boat without a ticket at this point. I said I forgot my ID and they just gave me the beer anyway without no hassle."

"I hate watching you eat." Stephen, still lying where he'd been asleep until a few minutes ago, grumbled from behind his balaclava. "It's like watching your best friend screw a gorgeous redhead while you're chained to a chair on the other side of a window."

Bobby choked on the comparison, thumping his chest to get the food clear. His neck separated into dragons, a chunk of chicken fell into his lap, and it all re-formed too fast for his head to fall apart. "I could eat it down there, but it don't seem rightly like a good plan, since someone might actually notice I ain't wearing proper shorts."

"Take some."

"I ain't seen a good opportunity to. Nobody walks around with spare clothes in their pockets. It's all in their rooms."

Stephen snorted. "Since when does that stop you?"

"I don't need it, it ain't right to take something when you don't need it."

"Seriously? You're still going to cling to that morality?"

"'S'only one I got." The food suddenly tasted bitter for Stephen hinting to All Of That. Bobby sighed and resolved to think of everything that happened in Afghanistan as staying in Afghanistan. Like Vegas, only a lot less fun. He hadn't had any nightmares, at least. Not yet, anyway. "You gonna grab a meal tonight before we take off?"

"Yes, I am. If I don't, I may well get hungry enough to chomp on you."

"Shoot, that's pretty gosh-darned hungry. Don't worry, though, I don't think I'll ever get hungry enough to try to eat you."

"That's neighborly of you." Stephen sat up and went quiet while Bobby stuffed his face. "Man, I can smell them all. It's like the ship is one giant buffet."

Since he thought the same thing, Bobby chuckled. "You wanna stay on the boat until tomorrow night or fly on after you eat?"

"You said it's headed in the right direction, but it's so damned slow." Stephen huffed out a mildly annoyed breath. "While I'm prowling, check their maps to see if leaving now is potentially committing suicide. More than fourteen hundred miles is probably too much to go before your next meal."

"Good point." Nodding, Bobby shoveled the last bite of potatoes into his mouth and set the plate aside to finish his beer. "We might be screwed."

"Nonsense. The worst that happens is we wind up on some stupid little island in the middle of nowhere, eating raw fish and sleeping out in the open."

"So we might be screwed, then." Bobby grinned and felt like laughing for the first time since All Of That.

Stephen snorted. "Yes, we might. If it's too far, we can always go back to land and catch a flight. You and I can both ride in a cargo compartment, and I seriously doubt we'll have any trouble sneaking into one."

"Fair point, but maybe we can find another cruise ship after this one. I kinda like it."

"Imagine that. I'm shocked, I tell you. Shocked."

Bobby followed Stephen's gaze as he turned his head west. The sun had slipped down to the horizon, throwing brilliant orange and pink light across the sky. It drifted down, disappearing from sight.

"I will not kill anyone on this ship." Stephen unlaced his boots, ready to pull them off the second he wouldn't burn for doing so.

"Me neither, and I know you won't. Maybe you should graze a bit here and there to make it easier to resist."

"Yes, that's a good idea. I'm not sure I like this ship business as much as you do. No hookers, no slums, and too many people who'll ask questions."

"I bet they got hookers, just not the cheap kind you mean."

Stephen reached over and gave him a playful shove, the first time he'd done it since All of That. Then the sun disappeared and he shucked his clothes, down to the same shirt and boxers as Bobby. Breathing in the sea air, he wiggled his toes and stretched. "Don't wait up."

"Don't s'pose you'd drop off my dishes? It was kinda a pain to get them up here without being noticed."

"Yeah, I can do that." Stephen took them and stepped off the side of their perch.

"Don't do nothing stupid."

Stephen grinned broadly. "No, that's your job."

"Damn straight." With the vampire gone, Bobby lay back and popped off a single dragon. He tossed his mind into it and flew all around the ship, scouting. Plenty of people milled about and sat on the open air decks, some of them enjoying the buffet he'd collected his dinner from. Kids ran and shrieked, and this boat even had a pool.

He dove through the first door he found open at the right time. From sitting on it all day, they knew it headed west, but had no idea where to. At a guess, it would head halfway across the Atlantic to some island paradise, then go back to wherever it came from in Europe or North Africa. They could fly on from that pit stop and probably be okay. The ocean couldn't be *that* big.

He thought a map would be difficult to find, until he discovered the part with all the shops. A screen dominated one wall, showing the ship and its route. This boat started in Lisbon, Portugal, and had a destination of Ponta Delgada, a tiny island somewhere in the middle of the Atlantic. It had reached halfway between the two ports already, and had no stops listed between them. Instead of mileage, the route had been marked by days and hours. Three days from now, it would reach the island, which might be a good place to rest and stock up on supplies before crossing the rest of the ocean on their own.

The shops sold most anything a body could want on a trip like this, and he found himself contemplating how best to take a pair of shorts without it being noticed. Out through the back of the shop would probably work. He summoned five more dragons and had them perpetrate a small heist of shorts, a shirt, and flip-flops. It was all necessary to fit in, because he intended to vote for sticking with the boat at least until tomorrow night.

Something started to annoy the dragons, and he had to land out of sight and focus to figure it out. They wanted to eat. When was the last time he let them eat? He couldn't remember, which meant it'd been too long. They messed up that car outside Elko, then...nothing. That happened two weeks ago. Dammit, he could've gone to Fort Morgan or Denver any time during that week before they went to Chicago. But no, he spent all his time with Lily and Sebastian, afraid of missing something with them. Stupid, stupid, stupid.

Right now, he could do nothing about this. Whatever might be found on the ship, he suspected letting them eat it might damage the engine or other important parts, stranding all these people out here. What would happen when they got really, really hungry? It seemed like maybe he'd find out, depending on how long it took them to get to that point. Hopefully, they could last three or four days. This island place probably had nothing for them, which meant they'd have to wait until he got back stateside.

On the way back to his body, he spotted Stephen, now somehow wearing a pair of shorts and an unbuttoned Hawaiian shirt. The vampire sat with a rather attractive blonde, talking to her about something. They both laughed. It must be nice to have that easy a time with seducing women. He said and did all the right things.

Then again, maybe he only knew how to pick the ones that would be receptive to a one night stand. He watched Stephen lean in and whisper something in the girl's ear that surprised her and made her cover her mouth. When he pulled back with a predatory smile, she gulped and nodded, nervously eager. They stood up and walked away, Stephen smug enough to peel a grape. Damn.

CHAPTER 10

"Bobby, I have to stop someplace, soon. I can't just go forever."

The dragons responded with chirps of acknowledgment so Stephen knew he'd been heard. They'd left Ponta Delgada at dusk yesterday and hadn't found a place to touch down for even five seconds since then. Twenty-four hours later, Bobby could hear the exhaustion in the vampire's voice.

The vast size of the Atlantic surprised him. He worried they might be flying in giant circles, they could have turned toward Antarctica by accident. While they had both the sun and stars to go by, he'd never navigated that way before and had no idea if they'd managed to stay on a due west course. He'd expected to find dinky islands dotting the ocean, at the least.

It'd been so long since they last stopped, he had no idea what to expect for the condition of his body. He'd never gone a full day without pausing to eat before. Worse, the dragons were cranky now, hungry enough to not give a crap about what he wanted. The second they found food, they'd devour it, no matter how much he wanted to stop them. Stephen would probably feel the same way by then, too.

What would happen when his body wanted to shut down for lack of food? What about the dragons? Was he slowly killing himself right now? Contemplating the possibility of accidentally starving himself to death gutted his morale, so he stopped doing that. He tried to, anyway.

"I think I'll be okay with blood, but I need to sleep." Stephen's voice did a much better job of breaking his downward panic spiral than Bobby's resolution to make it stop. "I'm not sure if I can drown or not, and don't really want to find out. Can you spread out to look for a place to land? Even just a little fishing boat would be enough."

Certain he could handle that, Bobby had the dragons trill. A third of the swarm streaked north, a third headed south, and the rest stayed with Stephen. Fortunately, they understood that food required land and cooperated with him.

Half an hour later, still with nothing in sight, the vampire slid downward. The dragons screamed at him. He woke up and held his head in both hands. "I'm just not up for two all-nighters in a row, Bobby, not without something more interesting to look at or do. Maybe I can float on my back? The water's pretty calm."

Great. Stephen would float on the current while Bobby did what? Keep going? Float with him? The dragons could keep going forever, so far as he could tell. Their little minds, though, had become consumed with hunger. He felt like hundreds of toddlers saying 'why?' over and over again had camped in his head.

"What I wouldn't give for some caffeine right about now," Stephen mumbled. His body bobbed up and down as he fought to stay conscious. Thankfully, the dragons could see the value of keeping the vampire going, and did what they could to help: chirping in his ears when he started to fall. Even so, they gradually drifted downwards. When they reached a few feet above the surface, Stephen finally fell in. Hitting the water only woke him up enough to roll onto his back, then he passed out again.

The dragons converged on him, no longer watching for anything in particular, and struggled to keep him from sinking under the surface. It overrode their hunger. Briefly. They came together, re-forming his body against his will, and Bobby realized with horror that he'd pushed them too far for too long. Usually, he did that fast enough to not consider the process. This time, it took them about a minute to do it, and he registered the exact point when his mind snapped into his head.

He slipped underwater and struggled to break the surface again, then thrashed about to reach and grab hold of Stephen. An all-consuming hunger hijacked his head as he did do, twisting his insides into knots of agony. His eyes drooped and his leaden limbs refused to cooperate. The dragons could go without sleep, but Bobby couldn't. The next time they did this, they'd take a plane, dammit. Because there would be a next time. Somehow, despite his gross stupidity, they'd survive this. Somehow.

Sputtering on salt water that he kept swallowing when his will to remain conscious wavered, he tried to relax with his arm looped through Stephen's. He blinked and caught himself coughing again. Any minute now, he'd slip under the surface for the last time, too weak to push his way back up. Karma caused this, he figured. For his crimes, he'd drown in the middle of the Atlantic, which he'd failed to grasp the vastness of.

In the middle of a disjointed prayer for God to watch over his Momma, he caught some kind of strange sound chugging closer. In his current state, he couldn't comprehend it well enough to attach a label to it. Momma shouted, saying something about water.

He thought he blinked, then he fell onto something hard. Faces swam in his vision. Momma told him to wake up and spit the water out. Rolling to his side, he coughed and thought he saw Stephen. Either he'd died or he'd been pulled onto something that would keep him from drowning. Assured the matter had been settled one way or the other, he closed his eyes.

When he opened them again, he groaned. His belly had wrapped itself around his spine and squeezed, making everything hurt. "I died," he gasped. His body curled into a ball of its own accord.

"Take it easy, Bobby, we're relatively safe. There's some fish, it's cooked. I can feed you, but you have to help me out a little."

"Where?" Without opening his eyes, he opened his mouth. A forkful of food pushed in, and he marshaled every ounce of willpower he had to take the time to chew it up before swallowing. Nothing had ever tasted so good as that bite of fish, a food he usually avoided.

Stephen fed him several more bites before answering. "A private yacht. The owners fished us out of the water and are headed back to port. The boat isn't very fast, though, and they were a fair distance from land. I've only had a short nap. When I woke up, I met them both and told them I didn't remember how we got where we were. I suggest you go with that, too. They think we're Army, I haven't tried to correct that."

"They call?"

"No. They were out in international waters and didn't want to deal with whatever the military might send out. Besides that, they were apparently headed back anyway, something about running low on food and water. It's a very nice older couple. We're in one of the bedrooms on their very nice boat. They sometimes bring their grandkids out with them."

The fish put a dent into Bobby's hunger. Not a very big dent, but a dent all the same. It let him relax and think about other things. "Dragons won't come out 'less there's food for 'em. They done starved, too."

"Understood. We'll have to be careful, then." He sighed wearily. "I need to get some more sleep before we hit land, Bobby. There's a bowl of oatmeal here, an apple, and a glass of juice. Also, the envelope is mostly okay. There's some water damage, but it's still all as legible as it was before."

"'Kay." Finally opening his eyes as the bed shifted under Stephen's weight, Bobby found himself in a bedroom. Everything had a nautical theme with a dark blue background. Their uniforms had been draped over every available surface to dry. He mustered the energy to sit up and finish off the fish and devour the rest of the food. It gave him enough to feel a more normal level of hunger. Given the choice between finding more food or getting more sleep, though, sleep won.

A knock on the door woke both of them. Stephen sat up as the door opened. It was a woman with white hair up in a bun, wearing a light blue shirt and white pants. Bobby rubbed his eyes and propped himself up on one elbow, thinking she must be sixty or so.

"Boys, we're about twenty minutes out from the marina, it's just past noon in Myrtle Beach. Denis is wondering if you might be up to helping us dock? It's just holding ropes and that sort of thing." Her light Southern accent made Bobby feel like he'd come home.

Stephen smiled. "Yes, ma'am, we'd be happy to as soon as we're dressed."

"I'm glad you're both okay."

"Thank you kindly, ma'am," Bobby managed to get out. "We're pretty happy about that, too."

She chuckled. "I'm sure you are. Just come on up when you're decent." Backing out, she shut the door again.

"Ma'am," Bobby muttered, "I ain't been decent for near on a week already."

"It's been a lot longer for me." Stephen grabbed clothes and pulled them on.

Rubbing his face, Bobby sat up and ignored his belly rumbling. "Did we make the right choice, leaving instead of staying?"

"How many bodies did you pile up again?"

"Yeah, you got a point." Scratching what had become a full beard while he'd been busy, Bobby sighed. "One good thing about this whole stupid flying across the ocean thing: it feels like that happened a million years ago."

"I hear you. I know I said otherwise at the time, but that cruise ship was a good idea. Made for some pleasant detox. And we didn't even kill anyone." He said it with a grin. Dark brooding lurked underneath. "Thankfully, Joan there isn't really enticing to me, so I haven't had to worry too much about the Hunger taking over. I'll need to hit something before we go too far, though."

"You can do that while I hit a junkyard."

"Yeah, good deal. I'm sure we'll be able to find one not far from here. I can carry you there."

"From there, we head for...did we decide?"

Stephen tucked Hanamidi's envelope into his coat and buttoned it up. "Not really. Either Albuquerque or the farm. I suggest we hitch on a plane."

"I'm good for that. Let's do Albuquerque and figure from there."

CHAPTER 11

Myrtle Beach didn't have a junkyard, but another town just up the road did. Stephen dropped him off inside, then went off to find his own food. The dragons descended on that place like a plague of locusts, tearing through it with delight and fervor. They spent a full hour diving in and under and through, chomping and chowing. Poor guy who owned the place got ripped off something fierce. One more pile of crap on his soul, if he even had one.

They met back up and flew to Columbia, where Bobby grazed on dumpsters before they sneaked through the airport and onto a plane bound for Dallas. He stayed in the swarm for the flight in the cargo compartment. Stephen stretched out on the luggage and took a nap. The next plane to Albuquerque kept them waiting for a few hours.

Another hour after their second flight landed, they found Adesha Wahiz's house. The neighborhood made Bobby smirk. Half the houses all looked the same and the other half were really, really different. It'd probably been built a while back by folks with all different ideas about what a house ought to look like. Then, some time recently, other folks came through and bought some of them, knocked them down, and replaced them with faux adobe, 'properly Southwestern' houses.

Adesha lived in a faux adobe one, of a not-quite-peach color. It had cacti and rocks for a front yard and a small courtyard space in front of the door. Keenly aware they still wore military uniforms, Bobby opened the gate and led Stephen to that door without hesitation, where he rang the doorbell. At least they didn't have guns. That would probably send a much worse wrong message.

All the way here, neither broached the subject of how to handle this conversation. Bobby pondered it briefly, only able to think of the worst possible way: 'Hi, we killed your dad, and he wanted you to have this!' He glanced at Stephen while they waited for someone to answer the door. They'd crossed into shade, so he pulled his headgear off, and Bobby snatched his hat and sunglasses off, too.

The door cracked open, the woman inside holding it open while bracing it with her body. She looked them over, her brow furrowed and eyes suspicious. Bobby could see Hanamidi in the straightness of her nose, and a little around the chin. The woman in the pictures he figured for her mother showed a lot more.

He threw on the most pleasant, friendly smile he could manage. "Howdy, ma'am. We're looking for Ms. Adesha Wahiz."

She let go of the door enough to cross her arms defensively. "That's me. What do you want?" For some reason, he'd expected her to sound Afghan like her father. Instead, she had a hint of a Southwestern twang.

"Well, I'm not sure how to paint this nice. I'm sorry to inform you that your father passed a few days ago."

Adesha narrowed her eyes. "Is this some kind of scam? He's been dead for years."

Bobby glanced at Stephen, who shrugged and produced the envelope from inside his coat. "Welp, he put your name on this here packet, at this address. We just figured you must be his daughter." Maybe he'd faked his own death? Bobby shrugged and pressed on. "At any rate, this is addressed to you, and we were kinda hoping you might be willing to tell us what the notes are about."

She took the envelope, expression clouding over as she ran her fingers over the writing on the front. "You looked through it?"

"It wasn't sealed," Stephen said. "And everything got wet on its journey here. We made an effort to dry the papers for you."

Tapping a finger on the envelope, she looked them both over again, then opened the door wider. "Come in and sit down while I look it over. If I can tell you anything, I will."

"Thank you kindly, ma'am, we appreciate it." They followed her inside the well-appointed and clean house to sit on plush couches, both choosing to perch on the edge rather than sink in and get comfortable. Watching her pull the papers, Bobby found himself fidgeting, like her opinion or reaction or something mattered more than anything else.

"This is his will, this is my father's name." Adesha sat down across from them in a matching armchair, confused and upset. "Where did you find this? Are you sure he died just a few days ago?"

"Yes, ma'am, it was found in a town in Afghanistan, along with him." He wanted to tell her the truth, as much of it as possible. If anything happened to his Momma, he'd want that courtesy.

Shaking her head in disbelief, she said, "I thought he was already dead. Nothing from him for years. What about my mother? Was she there?"

"I'm sorry, ma'am, we got reason to believe she passed a few years ago."

"Huh." Adesha frowned as she leafed through the pages. When she found the pictures, she flipped through them and stopped at one. "He was a scientist, worked on some top secret government thing. We used to ask him what he did, and he'd tell us silly things like 'looking for worms'." She set the pictures aside and scanned the notes.

Bobby scoured all the corners of his being for every scrap of patience he could muster. The woman needed to take her time and deal with this stuff. At the same time, he hoped she took forever. Once they got what they needed from her, they'd go back to the farm. Screaming and yelling probably awaited them, then lectures and cold shoulders.

"I guess he wasn't lying." Adesha sounded both amused and surprised as she looked up, papers in her lap and hand and the arm of the chair. "This is about wormholes. Unless I'm mistaken, he was working on the idea of interdimensional travel. He calls it out as an absolute possibility, starts from that basis. There was an event that convinced him it was possible, and he had data he was trying to use to re-create the event. He never succeeded, but thought he was getting close when he finally gave up and retired."

Stephen leaned in, looking more keenly interested than Bobby felt. They already knew this part, after all. If they acted like they knew it already, though, she might clam up. "Why did you think he was dead?"

She sighed and slumped her shoulders. "They lived in Alamogordo. He worked at White Sands Missile Range, so too far to see all the time. I used to talk to my mother a few times a week. One day, she just stopped calling and didn't answer her phone.

"My husband and I drove out there to check on them that weekend, and we found the place trashed, like someone went through everything. The police investigated, or said they did, and never found any evidence of what actually happened to them. After a few months, we assumed they were taken by someone and killed. That was years ago."

Bobby shared a glance with Stephen and knew he thought the same thing: if he worked at White Sands, maybe the project was still there. Also, Hanamidi's bosses didn't mess around, so they needed to be careful poking around this stuff. Kurt Donner had, more or less, suffered the same fate, after all. This sort of thing happening two separate times suggested some unpleasant things.

"That's a crappy thing to have to deal with, ma'am, I'm real sorry you had to go through that."

Adesha nodded. "Do you know how he died?"

"It was quick and painless." Thank goodness Stephen answered right away, because Bobby would have sat there looking guilty and probably given the whole thing away. "We don't know anything about your mother." He stood up, apparently convinced they had all the new information they were going to get.

Taking the cue, Bobby stood, too. "What're you gonna do with them notes?"

She looked down at the pages. "He wanted me to put them on the internet. I guess I'll do that."

"Be real sure before you do that. There's folks what might not appreciate it."

Nodding, she set the papers aside and also stood. "Yeah. I'll talk it over with my husband first. Thank you for bringing this to me. If for no other reason than so I have the pictures."

"Thanks for taking the time," Bobby nodded. Adesha showed them out, and neither said anything until they'd turned up another street and lost sight of her house. "We were gonna head for the farm now."

"We're really close to the missile range, though. Its just south of here."

"Yeah." They both stopped. Stephen leaned against a lamp post. Bobby crossed his arms and scuffed his boot on the sidewalk. "I ain't keen to go back."

Stephen snorted. "I keep thinking about how much we're going to be bitched at for having done this."

"That pretty much covers it. If'n we go back now, though, we can maybe have a better chance at White Sands, on account there'll be more talents to choose from."

"There may also be more chances for things to go wrong because of more people being involved." The vampire sighed and stared off at nothing in particular.

"Maybe we oughta just go back and get the tongue-lashing done with. At least we got something to show for it." It seemed to Bobby like both choices sucked. "I guess there's something else to consider, which is that the suits gotta know we bailed by now. They might be expecting to see us at White Sands. It's been near on a week since we left already, and that's plenty of time to set up for us here, just in case."

Stephen sighed heavily and straightened away from the post. "Fine, fine, we should just go back. I suppose it's not that far anyway. I want to see Kris before I deal with the rest, though."

"Coward." Bobby gave the vampire a flat look, because he knew that meant he would go back first, by himself. "After I done pulled your ass outta the fire, and you did it back, more'n once, you're gonna bail because of a little social pressure?"

The vampire made a little whiny noise. "I don't like dealing with angry women."

Bobby snorted and started to laugh. He couldn't help it. "Big, bad vampire is scared of girls yelling at you? Really? Mr. I Am The Monster In

The Shadows don't wanna get bitchslapped."

Stephen scowled. "Oh, shut up."

He gave Stephen a mock glare. "If'n you think I'm gonna let you go off to get laid in Denver while I face the firing squad, you're nuts."

"Fine, fine, let's just go before I decide to try and eat you."

"Yeah, it'll be 'trying'. Let's see them fangs work on metal." Still chuckling, Bobby broke apart into dragons spiraling upward.

ASIDE – CAMELLIA

When the two men got far enough away to not notice her even if they looked back, Camellia stepped away from the wall she'd been leaning against and let her body's camouflage fade away. She pulled out her phone and hit the speed dial on the way back to her rental car.

"It's Camellia. You were right, they came here."

"What did they do?" Privek sounded like he always did: sharp, focused, crisp.

"They went inside and talked to Adesha for maybe ten or fifteen minutes, then left."

"Did you hear anything?"

"Yeah." She took a deep breath and hoped she hadn't joined the wrong team. Privek and his people rescued her from those suits, but all she had to go on was the video and what he said. Whether Mitchell and Cant and the others really did all that damage for the reasons Privek said they did, she had no idea. Still, they were obviously capable of causing plenty of harm. That made them a particular kind of dangerous, no matter what.

"They're going to someplace they called 'the farm', and expecting to be yelled at. They're also planning to go to White Sands Missile Range, but not until they go back to that farm place."

"Did you get any impression for where this farm is?"

"Kind of. They went north, and said it wasn't far. Mitchell mentioned Denver, but like it's nearby, not where they are." She decided not to pass on the name 'Kris', on the off chance Privek would tear Denver apart and ruin all kinds of normal lives to find her. Even if it would help, she'd be pissed if he harassed her friends, and assumed they'd feel the same. "What do you want me to do?"

For several seconds, she heard something tapping. Maybe he fiddled with a pen or pencil while he thought. "Was it due north?"

"I'm not a compass, Privek, I'm a chameleon." She went ahead and gave the car an annoyed glare even though he couldn't see it. At least he could probably hear it.

"Could you follow them if you left now?"

Shading her eyes, she peered at the last place she saw them in the sky. That dark spot and collection of glinting flashes around it was probably them. She wondered if they followed roads to navigate, or had some weird, innate sense of direction. Chelsea said she could always somehow tell north. "I doubt it, they're pretty fast and I don't know the roads very well."

Another pause let her hear clicking noises might be him tapping keys on a computer. "Go to White Sands. Wait inside the base. Whoever shows up, follow them around and try to hitch a ride back with them. If you can't, call me when they're gone."

She unlocked the car and slid into the driver's seat. "Will I be on the access list, or do I have to sneak inside?"

"You'll be on the list. If you're not, tell the gate guard to call his supervisor."

"Understood." The impulse to chuck all this and go home lurked in the back of her mind as she hung up the phone. In six or seven hours, she could be back home in Phoenix. Now that she had this weird superpower, no one would find her if she didn't want them to. Her brother missed her, and she missed his stupid puns.

She started the car and thought again of the footage she'd seen. Soldiers had shot themselves, things had spontaneously blown up, people had had arms ripped off. Men as dangerous as those two and their friends needed to be stopped. Normal people had no chance against them. She'd agreed to do her part to take them down because she believed it needed to be done. With a heavy sigh, she checked her purse and pulled out enough money to grab something to eat. At least she could get authentic Mexican food around here.

CHAPTER 12

Bobby and Stephen landed together at the far end of the driveway. The sun had gone behind the mountains in the distance about five minutes ago, putting them in twilight. Stephen pulled off his balaclava, hat, gloves, and sunglasses, stuffing all of it into pockets. Bobby tucked his own sunglasses into his breast pocket. They set a slow, unenthusiastic pace up the long drive.

"I'd suggest sneaking in, but I'm starving." Bobby's belly rumbled to punctuate the statement as truth.

"Damn you and your stomach," Stephen smirked. "Someday, it'll get us both killed."

"Got close already, not sure I wanna test if it can do the job proper-like."

"Do you have any brilliant idea for what to tell them?"

This last flight took nearly four hours. Both of them had had plenty of time to think about it. Bobby had ignored that in favor of enjoying the flying. After starving the dragons by being stupid, he thought they deserved a little time with his head not annoying them. "I'm thinking we should go real light on details. They don't gotta know what all we done, just the important parts."

"Agreed. They especially don't need to know about Hanamidi or the caves. Or anything else after that, really."

"No, they surely don't." Bobby nodded emphatically. "If'n I could think of a way to put it, I'd say they don't need to know we was in that country at all. Not rightly sure how to explain the uniforms without that part, though."

Stephen sighed. "No, we'd have to lie to do that, and I don't think we should do that, not to them."

"Ayup."

They reached the house far sooner than he wanted to. All the cars sat parked in a row, and the front porch light shone in the gathering darkness. Bobby stopped where the two parallel lines of trees flanking the drive ended. So did Stephen.

"Look, whatever happens in there, I think we done the right thing more'n we done the wrong thing. Ain't nobody was doing nothing, and we done something. It didn't work out as great as we hoped, but we got something, which is more'n nothing."

Nodding, Stephen clapped him on the arm. "Well said." From the way a grin lurked around the edges of his mouth, Bobby suspected he meant the opposite and rolled his eyes.

As they stood there, stalling, Andrew stepped out the door and immediately lit a cigarette. The Creole relished the first drag he took, eyes closed in ecstasy.

"Guess we might as well get this going." Bobby reluctantly forced his legs to move.

Andrew's eyes snapped open and he peered around. "Who's there?" He called it out loud enough for anyone to hear him through the nearby open window.

"No one of consequence," Stephen responded.

Movement on the roof attracted Bobby's attention. "Thank God you guys are back." Matthew flipped himself down to the ground, landing with a soft thump. He paced over quickly and gave Stephen a brotherly embrace, then clapped Bobby on the shoulder. "They've been harping on me since I spilled, and that was the morning after you left. It's like having a bunch of cats watching you all the time."

Bobby chuckled. Stephen snorted. Andrew approached, smirking as he flicked ashes off his cigarette. "Did you boys at least get something worthwhile?"

"Yeah. Where's Hannah?"

"Meeting room." Andrew pointed with his lit cigarette. "With Alice and Violet. Kaitlin's in there, too. Lily's not. Everyone else is either out in the woods or screwing. You hungry? Soon as I'm done here I can warm up some leftovers for you."

"Starving," Bobby nodded gratefully. "That'd be great, thanks."

Andrew took a step back to blow his smoke away from them. "Sure thing, Bobby. Just watch yourself, don't talk stupid."

Matthew grimaced. "I'll stay out here. Already taken enough, thanks."

"I'll be up after," Stephen nodded to the werewolf.

"Right. Time to go get ass-whupped." Squaring his shoulders, Bobby marched himself to the front door and walked in without knocking. Voices buzzed from different parts of the house, too quiet to be understood. Pulling off his hat as a form of contrition, he stepped into the doorway of the meeting room and put on his best smile.

Hannah, Kaitlin, Alice, and Violet all looked up from their separate seats. They must've heard Andrew, at least, but all four seemed surprised to see him. Maybe they expected an encyclopedia salesman or something.

"Hi," he said with an uncertain wave. He scratched the back of his neck awkwardly.

Behind him, Stephen also stepped into the room. "Not interrupting anything important, I hope?" He sounded about as fake with cheer as Bobby felt.

"Bobby! Oh my god!" Alice jumped up and threw her arms around him, giving him a firm squeeze of a hug.

Kaitlin shrugged and returned her attention to her laptop. Hannah and Violet both stood and scowled. The former put a hand on her hip and the latter crossed her arms.

Alice let go and slapped him hard enough to knock his head aside. "You ass! What were you thinking?"

Stephen coughed. It sounded like a stifled laugh. "Matthew explained?"

"Yes," Hannah snapped. "Nice leaving him here to carry your water."

Bobby rubbed his face. He could live with Alice slapping him. "We got some stuff, at least. It weren't a waste."

"You're not Head Cowboy here, Bobby." Hannah glared at him. "It was your idea in the first place that we shouldn't go off and just do what-ever without the rest of the group agreeing to it. I mean, really, I can under-stand Stephen haring off, but I would've thought you'd be against some-thing like that."

Glancing back, Bobby got the distinct feeling the vampire decided not to be offended by that in favor of not getting blamed for this. At least he'd come along, but still. Coward. "It weren't like that." Even to him, he sounded whiny. Time to cut that out. "Look, do you want to know what we got, or don't ya? 'Cause we can spend an hour telling Bobby how he's a dumbass, or we can go straight to how it weren't a disaster."

"I think they should apologize to everyone." Violet reminded him of Momma. Maybe it was just her heavy Alabama accent, or maybe it had more to do with that stern, no-nonsense tone. He could almost imagine her saying 'don't you sass me, boy'. "For being arrogant, self-righteous dicks."

"Sure," Stephen said, "but that can wait."

"Yeah, we got a place to go." No, Bobby did not want to stand in front of the whole group and beg for forgiveness. If that would let everyone move on and get to work on more important things, he'd do it.

Hannah quirked an eyebrow. "Is that it?"

"We coulda just gone there and maybe had more, but figured maybe y'all'd like to know about it and maybe some come along. It's White Sands Missile Range. The Maze Beset project was there, or at least part of it was, and might still be. There was more'n one project under the name, all separate parts."

"Alright." Hannah's glare softened. "Come in and sit down, spill it."

"What's with the camo?" Kaitlin spoke without taking her attention away from her laptop.

Alice hugged Bobby again, then shoved him towards a couch. "They both look good in it, at least."

Bobby cracked half a grin and dropped down on the couch. "We were kinda in the Army for a few days, but that ain't important. They don't know nothing they didn't know before. We did a few missions for 'em, and run across a guy what knew some stuff." He explained what Hanamidi had told them, using the man's words. When he finished with that, he added his own thoughts and ideas from his discussions with Stephen.

"At this point," Stephen said, "it seems clear that we were created with alien DNA. It's a bit of a leap, but the evidence is piling up."

Bobby nodded. "I really do think somebody oughta break in at White Sands and see what there is to see, but it's got some risk."

"By 'somebody'," Hannah said dryly, "you naturally mean you two."

"We are fairly good at this sort of thing at this point." Stephen must have figured the worst had passed, because he leaned back into the couch and appeared to have relaxed.

"It don't gotta be us, but we're willing and got the skills and uniforms now."

"Hannah, I'm done—"

Bobby froze at that voice. He'd wanted to have a chance to change into regular clothes before she saw him. Turning to look, he found her staring at him in surprise, sliding into horror. Her eyes had gone wide and her mouth hung open, and she still took his breath away.

He gulped. "Hi, Lily." His eyes traced the lines of her face, wanting to etch them into his memory so well he never lost hope or his sanity again.

The room held its breath while she stared at him. Then she blinked and broke the spell, looking away to focus on Hannah. "I'm done with the towels, they're hanging in the basement. I'm going to bed. Good night." She turned on her heel and marched away.

His butt left the couch in a flash. As he reached the door, he heard Hannah say, "We'll figure this out in the morning."

Nothing else mattered except that when he hurried into the hallway, he saw her back. "Wait, Lily." He tried not to beg and knew he'd failed.

The words made her stop, giving him a chance to take a few steps closer. She crossed her arms and looked over her shoulder. "You could have left me a note."

"I know. I'm sorry."

"It's not just about me, Bobby, I had to explain to Sebastian. He thought you weren't coming back, and I didn't know if I should tell him otherwise."

He closed the distance and touched her arms, hoping for the best. "I didn't mean to make things hard on you." He'd told Momma that a thousand times, too. Somehow, he always managed to find himself needing to say it again.

He'd expected her to flinch, to haul off and slap him, to melt into his arms, to do something. Instead, he stood there and did nothing. "I'm tired, Bobby." His stomach chose that moment to rumble. "Go eat," she said wearily, walking out of his hands and away from him.

This time, he watched her go, wondering if he'd done worse than she could forgive. He took heart from her not slamming her door for half a second. Then he realized Sebastian must be sleeping already. Hanging his head, he sighed and trudged to the kitchen. He found Andrew setting a plate heaped with food on one of the picnic tables.

"She'll be happier to see you in the morning," Andrew said.

Bobby dropped onto the bench and shoveled food into his mouth. What had he expected? That she'd run and jump into his arms? Yes, actually. As stupid as that seemed now, he'd genuinely hoped she'd do exactly that. Obviously, he'd been a dick to leave without a word. Then he showed up in a uniform, probably reminding her of Sebastian, Sr. and how he never came home after putting his own uniform on. Dumbass. Stupid, stupid dumbass. Yesterday, this was the only place he wanted to be, and today, this was the only place he didn't want to be.

"Sulking is bad for digestion, Bobby." Andrew brought a glass of milk over for him. "I don't care if you eat that without tasting it, but you might. Best to pull your head out of your ass and pay attention to it."

"How long you reckon before she forgives me for being a dumbass?"

Andrew smirked. "Probably about as long as it takes for you to do something else stupid."

"So, just a day or two." It could have been a joke, but Bobby grumbled it, glaring at his food.

"Give or take, sure." Taking some pans to the sink, Andrew turned on the water and scrubbed them. "So long as you can accept it's your fault, I'm sure it'll turn out alright."

Bobby grunted and forced himself to slow down. The food, simple and bursting with fresh vegetables, surpassed everything he'd eaten lately. "Thanks."

"No problem." Andrew set one pan aside and moved on to the next. "My advice would be to ask John for some flowers to give to her. Not all women appreciate that, but she would. Best wait for morning on that, though. Far as I know, he's in bed already. Here's hoping it's with Ai, because I swear those two are driving me nuts with the looks and awkward conversations."

Though he found that funny, he couldn't muster more than a hint of a smirk. "I'll wash my plate and stuff."

"Don't worry about it, just leave it in the sink." He turned to go, but stopped and fixed Bobby with a particularly piercing stare. "Was it bad?"

"You could say that, yeah."

Andrew nodded. "Get plenty of sleep, then."

It was good advice. Bobby lifted a forkful in acknowledgment and farewell as the Creole left the kitchen. Not wanting to brood over food, he forced himself to stare at a knot in the table rather than think as he finished it. In his own room, he stripped the uniform off slowly, each piece feeling like a heavy load he could finally pull off and discard. With it, he was Mitchell, the freak who killed all those people for God and country. Without it, he was just Bobby. Was that how his daddy handled it when he came home between tours? The uniform did it, not him.

He balled up his shirt and threw it at the wall. That felt right, so he hefted a boot and hurled it as hard as he could. The other one followed, and within minutes, he crouched naked on the floor. Choking, gurgling noises filled his head and he grabbed his hair, trying to yank the death gasps out.

Had expecting her approval been the one thing holding him together? He bounced back up to his feet and paced back and forth across the tiny room. The walls closed in around him, too confining to breathe. Lashing out in frustration, he hit the wall with enough force that it exploded into dragons. Rather than pulling them back in, he flew apart.

The swarm surged to the window, yanked the screen out, and poured outside, spreading out and flying around like that would solve everything. He saw Stephen sitting on the roof with Matthew, talking. Light from the barn suggested Greg hadn't gone to bed yet. He might find Tiana or John out in the trees. But he didn't want other people, he wanted... He wanted Lily. After everything he did and saw and went through, he'd expected the hero's welcome and got the scapegrace's one instead.

A few of the dragons went to her window and peered inside. The curtain fluttered in a light breeze, giving him glimpses of her lying in bed, hugging a pillow. Well done, Bobby, well done—it only took him ten minutes to make her cry. The sight sobered him. He wanted to slip in there and wrap his arms around her. It was his mess, he ought to be the one to clean it up. How could he when what he also wanted to rip something in half?

He noticed Stephen give Matthew a hearty handshake, then take off straight up and head off to the southwest, probably for Denver. What he really needed was to exhaust himself, to make himself so tired he couldn't see straight. Alternately, he could beat his head against a tree trunk until he lost consciousness—that would work, too. It occurred to him that alcohol might also work, but he'd never been the type to drink that much at once.

Mad to get away from everyone and everything, he fled for the edge of the property. There, he landed and re-formed, and let out a primal scream, then another. A third croaked out with less force. Nothing changed, except his throat hurt and he had less of an urge to fly apart.

Standing there, he took in several deep breaths, letting them out slowly, just trying to calm down, to force away the memories, to get a grip. Maybe ten minutes later, he realized he'd come out here buck naked and broke apart into dragons again. It reminded him of the first few days after he discovered his power.

Having spent the last week or so on a sleep cycle that kept him awake at night, he had no interest in sleeping now and let the dragons loose to do whatever they wanted rather than try to deny he needed to settle. Some of them zipped through the trees, playing a weird game of chase, some dug around in the dirt, some hunted around in the trees, some found whatever surface they fancied and walked or rolled around on it. He'd never just let them do as they pleased outside of killing, and it surprised him to discover that they had different preferences.

"Welcome back, Bobby." Tiana's voice had him direct a clump to trill at her. "If you don't mind, the goats actually like to eat those plants you're digging up." The tall, slender black woman picked her way through the undergrowth towards him. Her hair, usually up in a tight bun, hung straight and loose with twigs and leaves stuck in it. The look suited her.

Bobby pulled the dragons up from the ground and figured she'd probably want to actually talk to him. If he could sigh, he would. Instead, he called the dragons back to re-form his body on the other side of a tree, out of respect for her more than any real sense of modesty on his part. "Thanks. And sorry. Here I thought I might go a full day before screwing something up again."

Her rich, rolling laugh invited him to join her. "Aw, I'm not all twisted up about you haring off like a half-cocked idiot. Otherwise known as 'being male'. Truth be told, I'm surprised you guys were the only two that ran off to do something. I would've thought Jayce would get a bee in his bonnet well before you two did. I guess he's got enough to keep him busy with lifting and moving things for Greg."

Grinning, Bobby huffed an amused not-quite-snort. "Yeah, well, he don't strike me as the type to come up with dumbass plans."

"No, I suppose he doesn't." She leaned against the same tree he'd squatted on the other side of. "Is there any particular reason you're naked and chewing up nature?"

With that question, all traces of amusement fled. "Stuff." He waved a hand vaguely, hoping she'd leave it alone.

"You want to talk about it?"

"No."

"Mmhmm." She stood there in silence for a few minutes. Neither of them said anything at all and neither of them went anywhere. It was kind of nice, having someone there without asking or telling or demanding or needing or wanting or judging. Stephen could do that. Stephen had gone off to get laid.

For some reason, thinking of the vampire made him think about All of That, and he discovered he had to say something. "We killed some folk, and it weren't real clear if'n we oughta or not. We done it on account Privek sent us to work with the Army. Saved some lives and all, but it's kinda messed up how saving lives can mean taking others away."

"You've killed people before, Bobby. Why were these different?"

"I didn't have to kill them. I coulda...just—" That felt like a lie. It was true in the same way that saying 'the sky is blue' is true: sure, it's blue, but 'blue' covers a lot of colors. "No, it's really not so much that I killed them, or how many, or the ones what didn't deserve it. It's *how*. The dragons went all rage-monster and—We found some soldiers, our guys, being held prisoner, and they'd been beat up and tortured some. It pissed me off, and the dragons too. We...ah...found a new way to kill. A few dragons climb down into a body's mouth, fly down, and punch their way out through the middle parts. No screaming, just funny gurgling noises and a little hacking."

"Wow."

"I ain't never seen lungs from the inside before, or a heart up close. I don't even know what all the parts I saw from in there were. And I can do a bunch at once, with hardly no noise. I throwed up after I done it to some three dozen guys in maybe ten to fifteen minutes." He peeked around the tree at her, afraid of what he'd see there. "After that, there was more, it was less...justified and stuff."

He saw her in profile, staring out at the trees with her mouth pursed up and eyebrows halfway up her forehead. "Damn, Bobby, that's...efficient. Something to be careful with. Do they know you can do that?"

His shoulders relaxed when she failed to freak out. "I don't think so. Them rescued soldiers mighta said something, but I doubt it."

"I wouldn't advertise it if I were you."

"No, that ain't gonna be my first choice for chitchat, never." He let out a breath he didn't truly realize he'd been holding. "The dragons, they...they're—I dunno how to explain this. They're me. Like a part of me what's wild and angry."

Tiana nodded thoughtfully. "You're not, though. You don't strike me as angry all the time. Maybe it's less you and more them than you think. You could try talking to them directly, explain your beliefs and that sort of thing. If they're part of your caveman brain, that might help."

"I dunno." He shrugged. "I never been scared of myself before."

"You're not a monster, Bobby. None of us are monsters. Some of us struggle with our humanity, but that doesn't make us beasts. The key is never to give up and stop struggling. So, it bothers you that you did something icky. Good. It should bother you. When the horrible things you do stop bothering you, that's when you've fallen off the cliff."

Put like that, he had to agree. "Making peace with it is my own damned problem, though."

"More or less." She paused and turned to look in the direction they both knew the house lay in, despite acres of trees between them and it. "Maybe you should talk to Matthew about it. He has less control over his killing, but he knows what it's like to have those kinds of awful regrets."

"Maybe." He sat down on his bare butt and leaned against the tree, staring up. "I had a girlfriend not too long ago what knew all the constellations and a bunch of star names. Looking at them now makes me think of Lily, though."

Tiana huffed out a laugh. "Don't even talk to me about your love life problems. Not interested."

"Fair enough. Thanks."

"Next time you want to talk, I'd prefer if you come looking for me instead of ripping up the woods."

"Yes, ma'am." Bobby let the dragons out again, directing the swarm back to his room. He grabbed a towel and got himself a shower, standing under the hot water longer than he normally would. More than dirt and sweat and salt sluiced away down the drain. Being clean improved his mood considerably, and he changed into shorts and a t-shirt, then went to Lily's room and knocked softly on the door.

Half a minute went by, leaving him wondering if she'd fallen asleep. Then she opened the door, her eyes red and cheeks blotchy. What he really noticed more, though, was how her shoulder-length hair framed her face, and how the nightshirt she wore hit her at mid-thigh and hung off her just right to hint at her figure. Her regular clothes were revealed more for fitting better, yet this somehow stirred his blood more.

Her eyes flicked from him to the door. He put a hand on it to keep her from shutting it in his face. "Just gimme a minute" he whispered. "Please?"

She sighed and stepped into the hallway with him, shutting the door behind her. "I don't want to deal with you right now, Bobby. I'm tired."

He reached up to touch her face, stopping when she flinched. Letting his hand fall again, he said, "You could wallop me a good one. It might make you feel better."

In a blur of motion, her hand flew. She slapped him so hard his head exploded into dragons. "No," she spat, "it's really not that satisfying." While his head reassembled, she ducked back inside.

"I'm glad we sorted that out," he told the door, trying not to be annoyed with her. The jerk stood on this side of the door; she'd reacted to him. Maybe Andrew had the right idea after all. Plodding back to his room, he dropped onto his bed and tried not to think about anything.

luck."

"Yeah." At least some folks here had decided not to hate him. He chose to consider that a win. Cracking the back door open, he listened to figure out who he might run across. It opened into the kitchen, from which he heard limited noise. Andrew hummed and talked to himself while he cooked, so he guessed it must be Sam making breakfast.

Judging the area safe, he walked in and found Sam stirring something that smelled like apples and cinnamon in a huge stock pot. Out of all the women in their group, she happened to be the one he wouldn't call 'gorgeous'. Though she had a tall, thin supermodel's body, he thought maybe her nose had been broken at some point and hadn't healed quite right, her blonde hair always laid flat, and a scattering of white chickenpox scars decorated her cheeks. Even with all of that, she still blew away any normal girl, like all the rest of their kind did.

Whatever 'their kind' turned out to really be.

"Hey, Sam." Peering deeper into the kitchen in case of bleary-eyed coffee drinkers hiding in the corner, he found the table empty.

She glanced over, did a double-take, then smiled at him. "Oh, hi, Bobby. When did you get back?"

"Last night. Can I get something to put these in?" He held out the flowers.

"Sure." She went to a cabinet and pulled down a metal cup, the kind used with a drink mixer. "This is about the right height, and it isn't really much use without the mixer."

"You ain't mad, then?"

Filling the cup with water, she shrugged. "Did you tell them where we are, or not take a chance to free the others?"

"No, I surely did not."

CHAPTER 13

"I really appreciate this, John." Bobby took a fistful of flowers from the Chinese guy who force grew them with his power, right in front of his eyes. He couldn't think of any way for John's power over plants to be used offensively (or defensively, for that matter), and kind of envied the other man for it. Obviously, if his dragons couldn't kill anyone, he wouldn't be in exactly this position.

John shrugged. "I'm still working on the whole 'figuring out women' thing myself."

With a heavy sigh, Bobby said, "I ain't rightly sure that's ever a thing you get to stop trying to figure out."

"Don't tell me that," John grimaced.

"Sorry. Um, how 'bout it's a thing you just get used to? I dunno." Bobby stifled a yawn and scratched the back of his neck. When the stupid birds started chirping this morning, he tried to roll over and go back to sleep. It didn't work. "I'm pretty much throwing everything I got at the wall and hoping something sticks."

"Plants are simpler, a lot simpler."

"I'm sure they are." Bobby realized he only kept talking to stall, so he raised the flowers and walked away. "Anyway, thanks."

John waved him off and turned back to his herb garden. "Good

She smiled more and took the flowers from him, stuck them in the cup. "Then no, I don't really see a reason to be angry. I hope she likes them."

Taking the cup, Bobby nodded and returned the smile. "Yeah, me too." He stood and watched Sam return to her pot. "Smells good."

"It's just oatmeal." She paused and stirred. "You're stalling."

"I'm hungry, though. Eating first won't hurt nothing." For once, his belly rumbling happened at an opportune moment.

Sam glanced at him, a bemused smirk turning up half her mouth. She said nothing, though, as she scooped him up a bowl and handed it over with a spoon. He sat down, set the flowers where he'd have to stare at them the whole time, and started shoveling.

"Bobby." He knew that voice well enough, and froze in mid-bite, bracing for a hard slap on his back. It hit with almost enough force on his shoulder to knock him into dragons. "I can't believe you didn't even ask me to come along."

Bobby swallowed and grinned up at Jayce as he got his own bowl. "Well, you know. I'm Head Cowboy, Hannah says so. Must be true."

"Mm. Cowboys and Injuns do not mix." The Native American man could out-hulk Stephen, and did so without the creepiness. He nudged Bobby with an elbow as he sat beside him. "You might have asked, though. Said something. Communicated your plan. Gotten feedback."

"Waited for committee assignments."

"I seem to remember *you* being the one—"

Bobby waved a hand to cut Jayce off. "Yeah, yeah, Hannah already done said her piece and she's probably still pissed enough to spit house-cats."

Jayce chuckled. "I will never get used to the colorful ways you have of putting things. Just when I think I've heard them all, out comes another one." He pointed at Bobby with his spoon. "None of this cowboy stuff next time."

"Yeah, yeah. I just done said I already got the lecture."

"I can hurt you."

"Not really." He smirked and got one in return. "Maybe a little. I can hurt you back, though, so we're even."

Bobby thought he heard Sam mutter, "Boys."

Jayce's eyes flicked to her, proving he hadn't imagined it.

"We gotta sneak into White Sands Missile Range next. I done turned over that whole thing to Hannah. She can figure who's going and who's not and what all." He burned to be in on that, wanting answers to his questions firsthand. The dragons, though might not behave well there.

"If it's all about sneaking, you're probably the only one who can do it. Maybe Tony." Jayce turned to his oatmeal and shrugged. "I wonder if the missing eleven all have sneaky infiltration powers, because a lot of us do pretty full frontal destruction." Jayce gestured with the back of his hand at the cup of flowers. "Trying to make up with Lily?"

"Something like that."

"I expect Sebastian will have her up shortly."

"Yeah." Bobby inhaled the last two bites of food and stared at the flowers, working up the nerve to try again.

Jayce waited two beats before he snorted. "Suck it up and do it, dumbass."

Bobby stuck out his tongue and grabbed the flowers, then stalked out of the room. While he would have preferred to keep stalling, now that Jayce knew, he had his pride on the line. Standing outside her door, he listened for the sounds of the boy, and heard nothing. In a flash of brilliance, he popped a dragon off his thumb and sent it inside to check if he'd be waking them or not.

The dragon flitted down to the cheap carpet, flattening itself as much as it could. It wriggled under the door, wings flat. One wing got stuck, causing it to struggle and then tumble out to lie flat on its back. He looked out through its eyes, and found her in the middle of changing her clothes.

He had a view straight up her sleep shirt as she pulled it off. That left her in lacy blue panties and nothing else. It'd been a while since he got to see any girl in this state of undress, let alone the one he wanted more than anything. Tiny dragons eyes traced the contours of her body, noting silvery lines around her abdomen and on the sides of her breasts that he guessed must be old stretchmarks. Her left hip had a brown mole. A spray of freckles graced her lower back.

Suddenly, she seemed so much more *real*. The imperfections made him want her more. He wanted to touch the lines and count the spots and kiss her everywhere and make her smile and gasp. Thoughts of walking and pulling her down onto that bed danced in his head until the dragon panicked and scrambled. The movement fouled his view and something forcibly snapped him back into his own head. He had to put a hand on the wall to keep himself from falling over.

She yanked open the door, face contorted with rage, and sleep shirt clutched over her chest. From the way she pulled up short, she hadn't expected to find him there. It did nothing to assuage her anger. Kicking the little crunched dragon out of her room, she shoved an accusing finger in his face. "If I ever catch you spying on me again," she growled, "I will never speak to you again." Her eyes flicked to the flowers and she shoved the cup so the water splashed him in the face and down his shirt.

His wits came back with the drenching. "Wait, that wasn't..." But she'd already shut the door. Yes, he was an incredible dumbass. Why did he not realize that was stupid *before* he did it? He could have just knocked. He *should* have just knocked. And he thought she was mad before. Now she had an even better reason to hate him. Yes, this relationship ended before it got anywhere. Maybe he was too dumb to handle a real woman.

He wiped the water off his face and let a handful dragons off to eat the crunched one. Three flowers had landed on the floor and he picked them up. Instead of going for a towel, he shucked his shirt and mopped up the small puddle on the floor. Jaw clenched in frustration, he retreated to his own room, two doors up. At the time Hannah offered it him, she'd done it out of kindness so he could be close to Lily. Just now, he saw it as a wicked form of accidental revenge.

Inside, he threw his shirt at the wall and used his towel in jerky, rough motions. When he pulled a new shirt on, he popped a seam, so he flung that one away, too, and just went without. As a sort of demented punishment for himself, he put the dropped flowers back into the cup and set that on his windowsill. It would stay there until he managed to accept that no matter how well he got along with Sebastian, he had no chance with the boy's momma. They lived in the same place and would have to deal with each other, and that's all they'd ever have.

On his way out the door to go find something physical to do, he walked into Christopher, who'd been about to knock on his door. "What d'you want?" he snarled.

"Honey, you're stinking up the whole place with how hurt and angry and just plain unhappy you are. I can help, if you let me." Chris's mild lisp and preference for other men made Bobby uncomfortable. The man's empathy made Bobby even more uncomfortable.

"Get offa me," Bobby snapped, aware he'd caused them to get tangled up in the first place. He pushed past the other man and stormed away, stomping out into the trees. Once he felt secure he'd been swallowed up by the forest, he picked a tree and smashed his fist into it. The pain from his crunched dragon compounded with this as he punched it, over and over. When it hurt enough to make him balk, he hit it one more time. His steam spent, he sat at its base and leaned against it.

Things could get worse, he knew it. Somehow.

"There you are," Hannah's voice accused.

"Yeah, here my dumb ass is. If'n you want to sling it for something, go right on ahead. I won't dodge or nothing."

She stepped into view. Since he kept his glare directed at the ground, he saw her feet in flip-flops. "I think we're going to send Lisa and Tony to the base. They should be able to handle sneaking around."

"Yeah, sure, whatever."

After a long pause, she stepped in front of him and crouched down. "Look Bobby, you broke your word and I don't trust you anymore. It's nothing more complicated than that. I didn't really trust Stephen in the first place, so nothing much has changed with him. But you, I trusted you. To have a level head, to put the whole group first, to not hide things from the rest of us. You broke all of that, every part. How am I supposed to send you to do this job when I don't even know if I can send you to fetch a book without turning it into a disaster?"

"Fine." He wanted to protest. She ought to give him a second chance. His skills would handle the job best. Nothing would get screwed up this time. The words never got far enough for him to open his mouth. Flicking his hand, he dismissed the issue, telling her without words that he wouldn't argue about it. No matter how wrong that seemed, he knew she had the best interests of the whole group in mind. Better that someone else handle it. He'd turned into a walking damned time bomb, or a killing machine, or something like that, and had no other use.

For a long minute, she watched him in silence. He picked at his jeans. Finally, she asked, "What kicked you in the balls?"

The question took him off-guard, and his mouth tossed out the answer before his brain caught up. "Lily."

"Ah."

He scowled. "I done it to myself."

"I see." She sounded amused, which annoyed him. "Why didn't you even tell anyone what you were going off to do?"

"I dunno." He shrugged and rubbed a fold of his jeans between his thumb and finger. "Everyone was just settling into a routine, like this is it, this is all what matters. Like having a place for us what didn't get scooped up is the whole thing. Even with Will here, coming back the way he did, it just didn't feel like nobody was even thinking about it no more. I guess I wanted to do something, and didn't want everyone to tell me it was too dumb or too risky or whatever."

She sat on the ground, crossing her legs in front of her. "Maybe you missed the freedom of being out there on your own, doing something that mattered."

"Maybe, I guess." That sounded very reasonable to him, and likely. He shrugged again, feeling that he must seem incredibly juvenile. "I wanna go down to the base, Hannah. I done a lot, and I ain't much good for sitting around no more. Ain't nobody here makes a better spy than me, and you know it, 'specially inside a building."

Nodding, she looked off into the distance. "I was thinking about your theories, and I agree with them. Which would make us some kind of government property, in a sense."

"Which means there's someone out there what thinks we belong to them and oughta be collected up."

"Probably." She patted him on the arm. "Pick someone to be your driver and take Tony and Sam down to White Sands. Add Lisa in if you want. I'd prefer if you pick somebody other than Stephen. Get whatever you can, but it's more important to go unnoticed than to get files or anything. Everything's probably electronic, so you might be able to carry it all on a thumb drive or something."

He finally met her eyes and gave her a muted smile. "Thanks."

"Good luck." She squeezed his shoulder and walked away.

Purpose rushed through his veins, a more potent drug than anything he'd ever tasted before. Hopping to his feet, he hurried inside, already certain about who he wanted to drive. He asked Sam to pack up a bunch of food, and would have done little more than grab a change of clothes if Kaitlin hadn't joined Sam in the kitchen. She sat with a bowl of pasta salad, picking out olives and artichoke hearts to eat them and leaving the rest of it alone.

It had been stupid not to come to her before he and Stephen left. It might have even been stupider than not leaving Lily a note. As much as he found her power creepy, she hadn't steered any of them wrong yet. This time, he had no intention of making the same mistake.

She, it seemed, felt the same way, because she waved him over and grabbed his hand when he held it out for her. "Blech, what a load of mush."

"Why're you eating them if you don't like them?"

She rolled her eyes and threw his hand back at him. "The future, dumbass, not the food. All I've got is 'mike'. I don't even know if it's a name, a microphone or something else."

"Anything we're s'posed to do or not do with it?"

"It's a positive thing, but I don't know how or why." She stuck her hand into the bowl and pulled out another olive.

"That's something, I guess."

"I get what I get, and that's all I got." She shrugged and ignored him in favor of the olive.

Getting up, he couldn't help but compare this prediction to the last. That one had been oddly specific. This one couldn't have been more vague, and he couldn't imagine how it would turn out to be useful. He left the two women with a wave and went to pack a change of clothes or two. Less than half an hour later, Jayce pulled their chosen car onto the highway. Bobby sat in front with him, and Tony, Lisa, and Sam shared the back.

Tony hailed from Miami, a Cubano who could shapeshift his body into a variety of inanimate objects, like tables and chairs and boxes and things. Sam came from New York City and could access computers and electronic things with her brain. Lisa was from Portland, a kindergarten teacher. Her superpower allowed her to access some kind of invisible space and store things in it, including herself. Someone else could carry it for her, which sounded plain weird to Bobby. As if he had room to talk on that front, though.

"It only took Stephen and me about four hours to fly from Albuquerque."

"You didn't have to follow roads or speed limits," Jayce answered amiably. "And we're going a bit farther than that."

"I s'pose it's for the best it'll be dark when we get there."

"Do we have a plan?" Tony had a light accent, one that hinted around the edges at his upbringing.

"Not really. Get in quiet-like, find whatever we can about Maze Beset or MB-02, get back out without being noticed, with or without hard evidence. I ain't never been there, though, so I ain't rightly sure how to set up a more specific plan than that. If'n one a'you has..." Bobby looked from one face to another, and all of them shook their heads. "So, I can do a scouting run when we get close, and we can figure something from there."

Sam ducked her head under her hoodie. "I found out I can...um...be inside an electronic device. If you can carry a thumb drive, I can go in without being seen."

"Good to know." Bobby looked to Lisa, who seemed very nervous.

"Clive—" Lisa's husband had proven himself capable by doing his fair share of work around the farm without complaint. "—says I'm about five pounds when I'm in the pocket."

"Dragons can handle five pounds, and a thumb drive. How about you?" He looked at Tony.

Tony shrugged. "I can't shift into something any smaller than half my size." The guy stood a few inches taller than Bobby and had about the same muscle mass. "A particularly large tumbleweed could get me to the building. I might be able to be a cart and get pushed inside, if we can just figure out which building to go into."

"I'll be in the car," Jayce smirked. "Bobby, maybe since you only have to carry a little bit, you can leave some of yourself in the car. If I'm going to need to provide a fast getaway, that would be good to know before you all come tearing out with an angry, armed escort."

"Ayup, I can do that. Not sure how many it'll take to hold up five pounds, but I can leave the rest here. Best not send in more'n I gotta anyway, just to avoid being seen."

Watching the scenery go by, Sam said, "I can sense you, like you're some kind of giant, busy device."

"Um." Bobby had no idea how to respond to that. "Okay. I guess we can experiment a little?" He popped five dragons off, and they flew to Sam, landing on her hand. As she stared at them, all five got really excited and looked up at her like she was a wonderful thing, and extremely interesting. Interested in what went on inside their little heads, Bobby threw his mind into one of them and found himself thrown into a conversation.

"—just doing what he feels is right."

"Sam, can you hear me? It's Bobby, inside one of the dragons."

"Yes, I can." She looked at his body and nodded, though Bobby couldn't see out of his own eyes right now.

"Good to know. We'll be able to talk, then." Jumping back out of the dragon, Bobby called his five back. "I can't hear nothing you tell them if'n I ain't in one of them. They're kinda all separate even though they're not."

"Yeah," Sam nodded, "I think I finally understand what you mean when you try to explain this."

"At least somebody does." Bobby turned around and settled in for the ride. A few times, he opened his mouth to try to start a conversation, but couldn't figure out what to say that wouldn't annoy one or more of them. His mouth shut again each time without a word, and the inside of the car felt tense to him.

They took turns driving to break the monotony. Bobby had a snack every time they stopped to switch. Jayce wound up behind the wheel again as the sun set and they passed a sign for Alamogordo. He picked a gas station and Bobby filled the tank while Jayce chatted up the girl working inside. When he finished pumping gas, Bobby dug into the cooler of sandwiches and polished off two before Jayce returned.

Inside the car, he opened a map he'd just purchased with the gas and held it up for everyone to see. "We can go into the National Monument here. You can fly across to it from there. Or we can take this road north and just claim we're lost when we reach the first person who wants to see some ID."

Sam pointed to some numbers written on the side in blue ink. "What's that?"

"The cashier's phone number."

Bobby leaned out and peered at the girl, judging her pretty in a normal sort of way. "You were in there for ten minutes and you got her phone number?"

Jayce shrugged. "It happens."

"Hmph." Bobby rolled his eyes.

Tony chuckled. "Man can't help it if he's got what the ladies want."

Lisa cleared her throat. "It looks like both choices are about the same distance from here?"

"I suggest the park." Tony tapped the monument on the map. "If we try to fake being lost, they may write down the car's plate number. Me getting out and walking around won't be strange, either."

"Sounds like as good a reason as any." Bobby shrugged. "Works for me. If'n you can't find a way through, on account of a fence or something, just go back to Jayce and wait in the car. I'll send one dragon with you, and if'n you need to turn around and go back, I'll know and it won't be no big deal."

"Good idea. I'll park as close as I can." Jayce pored over the map.

"My dragons can always find each other, so it ain't no big deal where you're gonna park. I can have that lone one with Tony lead him if'n he needs it."

With that possibility accounted for, they drove into the National

Monument. As soon as Lisa pointed out the sign declaring a per person fee for entry, Sam disappeared into her thumb drive, Lisa climbed into her pocket, Bobby dissolved into dragons and hid them all around the car, and Tony became a large piece of luggage. Jayce looked around the 'empty' car and chuckled to himself.

Pulling up to the ranger booth, he rolled the window down and flashed a brilliant smile at the woman inside it. "I'm sorry, sir, but the park is closed for today."

His smile faltered. "Are you sure? I'm on my way through, and I really just want to do the drive and get to Las Cruces for the night. I don't know when I'll be along here again. Please, I've heard it's really something to see. The preview is impressive," he gestured to the heaps of white sand on either side of the road that could easily be mistaken for snow.

She sighed.

He held up the cash and begged with his eyes.

The ranger blushed. "Well, okay." Taking the bills, she pointed into the park. "Just take the drive, though. I'll get into trouble if you go through the rest of it or get out of the car. Be out by forty-five minutes from now."

"I have no wish to cause you trouble," Jayce said gallantly. If he could have, Bobby knew he would've bowed. "Thank you for your indulgence. I won't waste it." The car trundled past her booth and he rolled up the window. "Well, that was fun. Maybe I can pick her up on the way out. Bobby, you wouldn't mind getting in the trunk, would you?" He grinned broadly while Bobby re-formed.

Unable to be truly annoyed in the face of that grin, Bobby snerked at him. "I ain't got nothing against you getting laid, but that kinda defeats the purpose of most of me staying in the car."

"Damn, I knew there was a flaw in this plan."

CHAPTER 14

After thinking about it more, Bobby did climb into the trunk and leave one dragon in the car with Jayce. The alternative meant that ranger possibly giving Jayce extra notice for the extra guy in the car with him on the way out. If she took a closer look, she'd notice his semi-conscious state and missing hand, and things would only get worse from there.

One dragon went with Tony. It took fifteen to hold up Lisa's invisible pocket and another one to carry Sam's thumb drive. Tony became a giant tumbleweed and rolled across the white dunes. Much faster than him, the rest of the dragons streaked ahead. He picked one of that group to hold his mind so he could talk to Sam as soon as they arrived somewhere interesting.

A fence marked the boundary between the monument and the missile range. Since it had no lights or cameras or patrolling guards nearby, Tony would be able to climb it and keep going. Rather than waiting in case that turned out not to be true, Bobby plunged onward over the weirdly white sand that reflected moonlight.

Two or three hundred feet into the base, the sand diminished, making Bobby think of water frozen in the act of sliding down a plain. Once he left the sand behind, he had trouble making out the contours of the landscape and stayed high to avoid hitting anything. Lights blazed in the distance, marking a cluster of buildings that he headed for.

As he approached, he saw that a handful of roads snaked out from the central hub, heading in all different directions. It had tank tracks alongside some of them, too. Considering how much secrecy surrounded the Maze Beset project, he suspected they housed it in a building flung out by itself. It would take hours to find the right one in the dark, even if he knew what to look for from the outside.

This middle part had the feel of a proper military base, and he picked the tallest building to land on top of, hoping they'd be able to find a map or overhear something, or randomly stumble across a useful person. He set both the pocket and drive down, then backed the small semi-swarm off and had them chirp all at once.

Lisa stepped out of nothing. Her fingers appeared, then her head, and she wriggled out. Sam's drive wobbled and spat out a stream of weird, silent lightning. The lightning outline Sam's shape, then she solidified on the spot. Between the two, Sam's made more sense to Bobby.

"What do you think?" Lisa did something with her hands, like folding a piece of paper, then she brushed them on her black pants.

Sam covered her mouth and belched. "I think I hate doing that."

Lisa patted Sam's shoulder. "I don't really know anything about scouting."

"Sam, we're going to look around. I'll be back shortly."

"Okay, Bobby, don't forget about us." Though still green around the gills, Sam smiled faintly at him.

"I'll leave one behind in case you need to move." He picked one dragon and sent it to Sam's shoulder. It danced around happily there. The rest of them spread out and flew through buildings, looking for anything worth investigating further. Having done this before, and with no expecta-

tion of finding anyone who fit the dragons' idea of a 'terrorist' around, Bobby felt confident they could be loosed to search for information on their own.

He found himself distracted by the dragon back with Jayce. It wanted his attention with something that confused it. Focused on the sight of the dragon he inhabited now, he tried to dismiss its concerns as something that could wait until later. When it grew insistent, he checked what that one could see and immediately wished he hadn't.

This poor dragon had no basis from his own life to understand what it saw inside the car. From its perspective, Jayce could have been in danger. It hesitated in defending him because that cute park ranger had been nice and friendly. Bobby wanted to smack his forehead. He settled for assuring the dragon that it had nothing to worry about. None of those moans had anything to do with pain and he could let the ranger be unless she pulled out a knife or other weapon. Later, when he wasn't trying to infiltrate a military base with only sixteen dragons, he'd explain. He could only hope that he'd get to demonstrate instead.

That handled, Bobby returned his attention to the more pressing problem of finding something useful and determining the security scheme. The ventilation system, as usual, gave him a personal key to every room, closet, nook, and cranny. The dragons flitted through the main base, noting minimal and sparse security. He feared the trip might have been a waste of time until he found a computer room with no one inside and only one camera that he felt confident he could turn enough to avoid it picking them up.

He brought the girls in through the vents and moved the camera. Sam commandeered a computer and let her fingers fly across the keyboard. The screen did things faster than her fingers moved, leaving Bobby wondering why she bothered touching it at all. Habit, maybe. In a few minutes, she'd cut through the security.

"There's a map here," she pulled it up to display on the screen and tapped it with a finger to indicate two of the outbuildings. "This one is MB-STA, this one is MB-02."

Bobby peered at the screen, fixing the layout in his mind. *"STA means 'Space-Time Anomaly'. We already know what that's about, and we ain't gonna find the others there. We want 02. Are you sure it's current?"*

"The file was last modified two weeks ago."

"Then let's go. Tony is on his way, he should be there shortly."

Orienting in the dark from the map he saw for only half a minute took Bobby a short time, then the semi-swarm plunged into the darkness with both women. It bothered him that this seemed too easy. Privek had to know they'd wind up here eventually, one way or another. The agent could even have set them up to meet Hanamidi so he'd have someplace to aim the gun, which would be right here. Wouldn't it?

The dragons found the building with Tony only a short distance away. Rather than waiting, they dove into the vents to see about unlocking the front door. For a location with a top secret project, it had little security: no cameras, no motion detectors, no guards, no fancy locks. He set the drive and pocket down and chirped. By the time Lisa opened the door, Tony had returned to his human shape. He slipped inside, Lisa shut the door, and they filled Tony in.

"This is weird," Sam said, sitting with her back to a wall and her hand on her belly. "There's almost nothing here." The rooms they'd found so far had empty desks, clear tables, and blank shelves.

"Maybe they just haven't gotten around to reusing the building yet, so they leave the old designation on the map." Tony opened an interior door and poked his head through it.

Lisa rubbed her arms. "I'd hate to have gone through all of this for nothing."

"We should explore the building."

Sam nodded. "Bobby's right. Let's split up and look around. There's obviously no one here. Maybe they left a computer behind, or some files or something."

The dragons fanned out, searching for anything of use. After spending at least an hour in the place, Bobby found nothing—no computers, no files left behind, nothing. Did he and Stephen really go through all of that for nothing more than some new theories?

"Maybe we should check that STA building after all."

Sam called out and the four of them gathered back in that front room, showing each other all the nothing they had found. "Bobby wants to check out the other MB building."

Tony shrugged. "You go, Bobby. If it's as empty as this one, no sense in all of us breaking in."

The dragon chirped his agreement and Bobby took thirteen of his dragons with him, leaving behind one for each shoulder in case they got separated. As his group darted out through the venting, he saw them leave the building and lock the door behind themselves. The other building also had minimal security. This one, though, had computers and books and papers and used coffee mugs. Bobby got his dragons to lead the others to him, then his dragons fanned out to search the site.

By the time the others arrived, he'd unlocked the door and explored most of it. Sam sat down with the first computer she found while Tony and Lisa poked through the other rooms. Bobby sent half the swarm with Tony while he and the other half followed Lisa, keeping watch in case he'd missed someone buried under paperwork in the back.

Lisa turned a corner and proved his fears right when she nearly walked into a man stirring coffee on his way out of a kitchen-like break room. He wore a suit minus the jacket and his tie had been loosened. She sucked in a breath and Bobby pulled all his dragons behind her and out of sight.

"Who're you?" He squinted at her, his mouth tugging down into a frown. She wore black leggings and a navy tunic-shirt belted at her waist with navy flats. She'd done her best at fulfilling his off-the-cuff suggestion of 'ninja expedition suit'.

She paused a beat too long before answering. "I'm Lisa?" Her voice shook. "Who are you?" Then she offered her hand to shake with him.

His eyes flicked to her hand, her chest, her face, and her waist. "Where's your ID?"

Bobby had no interest in hurting this guy, let alone killing him. The guy had no gun and presented no physical threat. No one deserved to die for the crime of working late. When Lisa hesitated and tensed, Bobby knew she couldn't handle this situation. He had to take control, dragon-style. The sub-swarm darted out from behind Lisa and into view, surrounding her head as a weird sort of halo.

The man's eyes bulged and he stumbled backwards, sloshing coffee onto his shirt. "Oh my God. *What* are you?"

Lisa looked from side to side and covered her face. "Oh my gosh," she whispered, mortified. "Bobby, what are you doing?"

Good thing he brought a kindergarten teacher along. The dragons surged at the guy's face, forcing him farther away from her. He dropped the coffee mug. It shattered and splashed hot liquid everywhere, making Lisa shriek and dance back. Bobby kept the dragons circling the guy's face to prevent him from grabbing hold of his wits, or pulling out a phone, or going anywhere else.

"Sam!" Bobby called out as forcefully as he could.

"What happened?"

Relieved he wouldn't have to go find her, Bobby tried to figure how to sum up the situation without sounding like a complete ass. *"There's a guy in the break room and Lisa needs help."*

Tony ran in. He looked around, blinked several times, and chose to grab Lisa and pull her out of the room. Fat lot of help either of them were.

Sam showed up, panting from the sprinting, and almost ran into the wall. She caught herself on the door frame. Bobby hoped that only happened because she'd gone too fast to stop properly. Instead of leaping in to do whatever she could, she scanned the room and stood there, staring.

Bobby wanted to smack his forehead again. *"Tell him to sit and calm down or the dragons will eat him. Hands out in plain sight."*

She gulped and nodded. "The dragons won't hurt you if you take a seat and keep your hands where I can see them."

Thank goodness she only needed to be prodded. The dragons backed off, giving the man room to breathe and follow her directions. They stayed close enough to dive in and do unpleasant things if he chose not to. *"You'll need to ask him about the Space Time Anomaly and MB-02. I'll help if'n you need it."*

The guy, darting his eyes from Sam to the dragons and back several times, put his hands up. "Don't hurt me." He edged to the seat and dropped down into it. "I'm just a software engineer, not a spy or anything. I probably don't know anything about whatever you want."

Sitting in the other chair, Sam rested her forearms on the table and leaned on them. "We know this project is about trying to reproduce a space-time event. What do you know about the original event?"

Bobby landed on the table, and the rest of his dragons followed suit. They formed a line in the middle, ready to defend Sam at any moment.

The guy gulped. "Almost nothing. My job is about data analysis and extrapolation. I don't have access to the raw data, just an exemplar set for formatting and ranges."

Frowning, Sam nodded. "Then can you tell us anything about the MB-02 project?"

"Sorry, never heard of it. I saw that's on the new map they distributed a couple of weeks ago. That building was empty before that so far as I know. I figured it was some new project thing they haven't set up yet."

Bobby currently had no stomach for the bottom to drop out of, nor did he have blood to run cold. *This is a trap. We gotta git.*

"Okay. Just one other thing." Sam took a deep breath and fixed him with a piercing stare. It had to be the most bold thing Bobby had ever seen Sam do. "Have you ever seen anyone, even in a photograph, with eyes like mine before?"

The guy blinked and stared at her eyes. "No. No one, ever. They're..." The intensity of her gaze must have bothered him, because he ducked his head and looked away. "Um, you have nice eyes. Nice to look at, I mean."

"Thanks. We'll go. I hope you don't get into trouble over this."

"Damn, me too. I guess if we all just keep quiet, everything will be fine."

"We didn't take anything," Sam said with a small, shy smile, "so there's no evidence if you don't tell."

The guy echoed her smile. If Bobby'd had regular eyes instead of robotic dragon ones, he would have goggled at the fact these two geeks tiptoed on the edge of flirting at a time like this. *"Sam, we gotta go. Sooner, not later."*

"Right." She ducked her head and shuffled out of the room. The dragons took off and followed her.

"Wait, um, wow, this is weird and awkward, huh? I'm Mike."

Despite the insanity of this encounter, his name made Bobby pause. Given what Kaitlin had said, they could at least expect him to keep quiet. Still, they needed to get out of here before the trap sprang. The dragons trilled at Sam and flowed around her, hoping she'd hurry up.

"Sam," she told the guy, then paused at the doorway. "It was nice to meet you. Sorry for the scare and trouble."

"Yeah. It's okay."

More dragon trills goaded Sam into moving again. With a last glance back at Mike, she hurried to the front door. Tony and Lisa stepped outside a few steps ahead of her and she pulled the door shut behind herself.

Too frustrated to be civil, Bobby had exactly nothing to say to any of this crew. Lisa stepped into her pocket and dragons picked it up. Tony's body twisted and squished into a giant tumbleweed and he rolled east. One dragon followed it.

Sam, though, stopped with the thumb drive in her hand and checked the door. It opened and Mike popped his head out, smiling like an idiot when he saw her. "Hey, um, can I give you a lift someplace?"

"Tell me you ain't seriously considering that."

A dumb smile of her own sprouted on Sam's face. "Yeah, that'd be great." *"Maybe he knows more and I can get him to open up."*

Bobby the dragon hovered and stared at her in disbelief. *"And maybe he's one of them and'll stuff you in the trunk if'n he gets half a chance."* When she didn't respond to that but did take Mike's hand,

Bobby's dragon rolled its eyes. *"Fine, but I ain't letting you go alone. Drop the drive and I'll bring it along, so we can have a getaway if'n it goes all wrong."*

She scuffed a shoe to cover the sound as she dropped the drive. Bobby scooped it up and watched her walk away from the small puddle of light outside the building with a random guy. He decided his mood would only get worse if he had to listen to them being nerdy at each other. The thumb drive in his claws, he landed on the back bumper of Mike's dark blue sedan and held on.

ASIDE – CAMELLIA

Privek had said they would come here, and they did, which made Camellia wonder how much he'd held back about these people. Probably a lot. Privek struck her as a guy who kept lots of secrets and rarely parted with one willingly. That, of course, didn't matter now.

They traveled in a highly unexpected way, and she had no idea how to follow them. Sure, she'd entertained the possibility it would be Mitchell and Cant again. They certainly knew how to get things done and weren't afraid to do it. Based on what they'd said in Albuquerque, though, she figured they'd be benched in favor of others who'd need a vehicle to get here.

It surprised her more that they went to the second building. Privek said to expect them at the first building, and to follow them out of it. He'd never mentioned a second site, not even as a vague possibility. She had no idea why they came to the base in the first place, let alone why they'd trooped from one building to another.

While they'd been inside, she'd considered calling him, except she had nothing to report. This qualified as a wrinkle, not earth-shattering news. Wrinkles needed to be ironed out at the time and dealt with. Her mission involved one thing and one thing only: finding a way to follow them to their compound so Privek could use the GPS in her phone to pinpoint it.

They spent a lot more time in this second building. Her jaw dropped when the employee offered the last one a ride. Those two obviously had some sort of something going on between them, even with only an hour or two spent building it up. Did men ever think with anything besides their dicks?

She watched them walk to his car, parked in darkness, and realized she owed that guy's libido her thanks, because he made it possible for her to follow them. Hurrying over, she noticed the dragon landing on the bumper. It carried...a USB drive? Interesting. Why didn't the woman just take that? For that matter, why not carry the dragon in her pocket or purse?

Never mind. The rear lights came on and she let the car back up past her. She waited to hop on until it hit the small bump between the parking lot and the road, hoping the jostling would cover it for her. Holding onto the spoiler, she made sure to keep her head away from the dragon so it wouldn't hear her breathing.

CHAPTER 15

Bobby had no interest at all in listening to Mike and Sam together. The guy somehow forgot the fact that he'd run into her while she'd been breaking into his workplace, and might be in control of a small quantity of tiny robot dragons. Didn't he have to get a security clearance to work on a part of the Maze Beset project? This completely explained every time he'd ever heard about governmental incompetence.

When they got out of the car, Bobby flew into Sam's pocket. If anything happened to her, he'd be there to help get her out of it. He settled in, worried about five hundred things going sideways, only to find himself listening to them using words he'd never heard before. They may as well have been speaking Swahili for all he understood.

He did understand when they ordered coffee and sandwiches, at least. From the noise level in the place, he figured they'd be here for a while. Any unpleasant surprises Mike meant to spring would likely come after the meal, which meant he could settle back and ignore them. Since he had nothing better to do, he threw himself back at his body to fill Jayce in.

For the first time, he felt something during the brief moments between dragon and body. It reminded him of falling, then he woke up in his body, in the darkness of the trunk. The distance must have affected him, since he hadn't tried it from so far away before.

After checking with the dragon in the car for nearby witnesses or the park ranger, he pulled the release to open the hood and climbed out to find himself in the back of a nearly abandoned big-store parking lot. Jayce had picked the one spot with a malfunctioning light, or he might have climbed up somehow and smashed it.

Bobby shut the trunk and stretched. Jayce stepped out of the car, holding a bag of food.

"Aw, you shouldn't have," Bobby said with a smirk, finding a fat, foot-long sandwich inside.

"I know, but I'm a nice guy."

"Mmhmm." With only one hand, getting the sandwich out, peeling the paper away, and holding onto all of it proved a challenge. For food, he could make an extra effort. "This ain't gonna make me forget having to deal with a dragon what didn't know heads nor tails about you getting some with that ranger."

Jayce blinked in surprise, then laughed. "Huh. Sorry about that. She asked me." His grin turned decidedly smug.

"You expect me to believe that after you talked her into letting us through the gate, when you left, she asked to jump you?"

"Of course not." Jayce snorted. "That's ridiculous. She asked me out to dinner. I just got creative regarding what 'dinner' entailed."

"And I got to watch," Bobby grumbled. "You know, I can't actually turn it off. I can ignore it, more or less, but I can't just not see it. Especially when the dragon wants to know if that lady is trying to kill you because you're making funny noises it thinks might be on account of pain. You're lucky it didn't just attack first and ask never."

Lisa returned, sparing him the indignity of being laughed at for several minutes. He got most of his hand back when that clump of dragons returned too, and he attacked the sandwich with fervor.

After checking around for anyone else and not finding them, Lisa bit her lip and asked, "Is Sam okay?"

"Yeah," Bobby gave a little amused huff, "she and that Mike guy are geeking all over each other."

Jayce smirked. "Is that what they call it in Atlanta?"

Reaching out, Bobby punched Jayce in the arm. It hurt, because even though Jayce had his own flesh for now, he still had more muscles in his wrist than Bobby had in his thigh. "I mean they're talking about computers and stuff. It was boring. She's hoping to get him to reveal he knows something else accidentally, but this whole thing was pretty much a big damned waste of time. Soon as Tony gets back, we should head to where she is."

"Sounds like a plan."

Lisa pulled a box of crackers out of her nowhere pocket and nibbled on them. "They updated that map two weeks ago. It's too bad we didn't look up a map from two weeks ago to see what they changed."

Bobby shrugged. "I got a feeling this was a trap of some kind, but it's a weird trap. I mean, ain't nothing been sprung I can see. We came, we left. What in heckbiscuits they hope to accomplish by having us do that?"

Jayce rubbed his chin. "They could already have the location of the farm. This might have been intended to lure some of us out so they could attack while we're gone."

Halfway through a bite, Bobby stopped and looked down at his sandwich. If the suits were assaulting the farm right now...he could do exactly nothing about it. It would take him at least five hours to fly up there, by which time it would be over and done. Besides, they left capable people behind, and Kaitlin should be able to warn them about anything major. Right?

Lisa blanched and put her crackers back away. "Clive is still there. They wouldn't hurt him, would they?"

"I doubt it." Jayce shrugged. "They've been more or less going out of their way not to hurt anyone but us. But they might take him to use as leverage against you."

"Oh, God. We have to go back."

"Yeah," Bobby said with a sigh, knowing exactly how she felt. "But not until Tony gets back and we pick up Sam." Resigned to being able to do nothing at the moment, he stuffed more sandwich into his face. The dragon accompanying Tony escorted him to the car a few minutes later.

"I guess it's time to get moving," Bobby said as his dragon reattached to his hand. "I can lead us thataway, and I'll go into that dragon when we get close to see how she wants to play it."

"Are you sure she's okay?"

Lisa's bright, earnest concern made Bobby wanted to pinch her cheek or pat her on the head. "If'n she weren't, the dragon in her pocket would let me know. If'n it couldn't, I'd know that, too." He gave her an encouraging smile. "I promise."

The drive took them to the other side of the town. When Jayce parked across the street from the little strip mall, Bobby flung himself back into the dragon and found the pair still talking about stuff he didn't understand.

"Sam, we gotta get going. Starting to think this was a setup to get us outta the way for an assault. Car is across the street."

He saw her tuck some hair behind her ear and incidentally look at her watch. "Oh, my gosh, the time. I need to get going."

"Oh." Mike's face fell. "Here's my email address, and this is my username, we should meet up in game sometime."

"I'd like that. Thanks for the nice time, Mike, I really enjoyed it."

"Yeah, me too. Can I give you a lift someplace else?"

"Nah, I'm just going to disappear into the ether." She laughed as she said it. Mike laughed, too.

"I sure hope that weren't the biggest mistake ever."

"So do I, but it was worth it. Now I have a contact inside the project."

Unconvinced but unwilling to belabor the point, Bobby went quiet. He noticed the trunk pop open and up for no apparent reason and sent some dragons to check it out. They found nothing, so he hopped out and tugged on the release handle in case it had gotten stuck. Slamming it shut gave him a tiny vent for his worry and frustration. He really needed a much bigger one.

He wanted to yell. Because he had no cause to sit up on a high horse with these people, he kept quiet until they hit the freeway. "Did you look up everything there is to look up on that guy?"

"His name is Mike." Sam pulled her hood up and shrank into it. "And no, not yet. I have his email address now so I can get into everything, I just need anonymous wifi to do it. I'll check him out when we get home."

"If there's a home to get to," Lisa said with a light edge of panic.

"The drive back will be just as long as the drive there," Jayce said. "We'll be lucky to get back before noon. Everyone should try to get some sleep so we don't have to stop on the way."

Bobby stared out the window. Jayce was right, of course, though that did nothing to make him tired. As much as he didn't want to think about what happened in Afghanistan, the place had a strange sort of certainty to it that didn't apply here. Klein pointed him at bad guys, and he killed them.

Granted, the 'bad guy' label had caused some problems, and he'd peered into the deep end of the pool there. Aside from that, the whole thing was really straightforward: identify, kill, move on. Stephen got professional about it, too. None of this fraternizing with the enemy stuff, not unless the enemy wasn't really an enemy. Or something like that. His own discontent confused him, yet again, and he let out a heavy sigh.

"Bobby." Lisa's voice startled him out of what had become a good brood.

"Hm?" He rubbed his face to wipe away all the thoughts bouncing around inside.

"Why did you throw all the dragons in him?"

Bobby bit back the impulse to snap at her. "Because he's a normal and coulda went for a phone to call security or somesuch."

"But he wasn't doing that. He was just standing there. You scared the petals out of him."

The odd turn of phrase made him stare at her while he figured out what she meant. "Uh, you can't just react to everything, sometimes you gotta do something before they do it first. Life ain't about sitting around and waiting for it to hand you some eggs so you can make an omelet, you gotta go find the chicken yourself and take them."

Lisa nodded meekly and turned away.

Tony, though, eyed Bobby. "Everyone was all surprised by how you took off." He gestured to Jayce. "They all said you were cool and relaxed, and it must have been that Stephen talked you into it. But they were wrong, weren't they?"

"You got something to say, come out and say it. It ain't like Hannah ain't already said it, I'm sure."

Tony snorted. "You're an arrogant brat."

"Fuck you." Bobby glared out the window.

"Well," Tony chuckled, "at least we know they're right when they say you aren't the sharpest tool in the shed."

"I can kill you." For once, when he said that, Bobby actually meant it.

Another scoffing huff came out of Tony. "Yes, a true gentleman and oh so concerned about the rest of us."

"Stop it," Lisa snapped. "We're all in this together. We should act like it."

"Tell him," Tony sneered, pointing at Bobby.

"Shut it," Jayce said cheerfully, "or I'll shut it for you. Bobby knows he screwed up. He doesn't need everyone reminding him over and over again. You'd be surly, too. Talk about something else."

The car went silent and Bobby glowered at the glass beside him until he nodded off. He woke with a start after a nightmare that left him with nothing but a deep sense of unease. The sky glowed with early morning light and Sam was driving. Afraid he'd startle her and cause an accident, he stayed quiet and still.

After a minute or so, she said, "There's still food in the cooler. It should be in reach."

The suddenness of her statement made him jump, waking him up better than a splash of cold water. "Thanks." He rummaged through the cooler and pulled some fruit salad and an unmarked sandwich out. "Wasn't sure if I was really awake or not."

"Sure." It sounded like she believed him. "I saw Lily before we left."

"I don't wanna talk about that." He devoured the fruit and moved on to the sandwich. Thank God for sandwiches.

"Okay."

This sandwich had lots of vegetables and some kind of paste in it. It tasted alright, and he had no cause to be picky. He bolted the food, trying to ignore the thoughts Sam's small statement had dredged up. He'd been an utter dumbass, and he knew it, and anyone she told probably thought worse about him than before. Given where he'd started, that almost seemed like an accomplishment, of sorts.

He licked his fingers and sighed. Sam had given him an opening to explain, and he needed to take it if he wanted to fix this. "It weren't like I was just trying to see her naked or nothing. If'n that's all I wanted, I woulda done it proper-like, with asking and groping and stuff."

"Why *did* you do it, then?"

"I didn't want to wake her up if she weren't already, and kinda got distracted when she turned out to be up and getting undressed already." He stared out the window to avoid seeing Sam's reaction. "It made sense at the time."

She choked down a laugh. "You're kind of an idiot, Bobby."

"Yeah."

"I'm sure if you explain, she'll forgive you. Eventually."

He shrugged. "I ain't." That hurt had only hit him yesterday, not even a full day ago, yet it already felt distant and faded. Leaving for this had done some good, at least. The hard part would be keeping it from affecting Sebastian. He liked the kid, liked playing with him and teaching him things. Liked his momma, too, but hecouldn't have her. Heckbiscuits, maybe that was even for the best. Dating a half-sibling sounded bad. Even if they never had any kids together, it would still always weird. "Don't matter."

"Sure it does. We all live in the same place, Bobby. We're a community whether we want to be or not. All of us feel the friction between people. Tony's a strident homophobe, which makes Greg stay away from the common spaces, even just to eat. We're all missing out on talking to him, and he's a pretty interesting guy. Plus, he's missing out on talking to everyone else. He now interfaces with the group through Albert instead of in his own right, just because being treated with such blatant, blind hate upsets him. In turn, I don't want to deal with Tony either, so we wind up out here together, and maybe I took a risk I shouldn't have, just because I was annoyed with Tony, even though he hasn't done anything specifically annoying on this trip."

Bobby slouched in the seat, unhappy with how complicated everything had to be. "It's like high school all over again," he groaned.

"It's worse than high school." She grinned. "It's *superhero* high school."

"I don't wanna deal with that kinda crap."

"Then why did you come back? You could have just stayed with the Army and kept doing their missions. If you stayed out there, you could probably end the war completely, one way or another. Or you could run off someplace else. With your superpower, you can probably get anything you want, and never need to work another day in your life. But instead, you came back. Even though you knew everyone would be angry, you came back. Why?"

"'Cause Lily." The moment he said it, the hurt came crashing right back down. It had been held back by a fragile dam of denial before. Also, though, he realized the truth had more to it. "And Stephen, and Jayce, and having folks what understand. Folks I can trust with my back."

Sam patted his arm. "Yes, that's exactly it. The farm is still pretty new. Give it a chance. And talk to Lily. Maybe wait until tomorrow though, when you've had a good night's sleep."

Bobby grunted noncommittally. He'd have to think about how to say what needed to be said. Because she was right, and he needed to admit he wasn't ready to let go of Lily, not even close. "I'll take a turn driving."

ASIDE – MAISIE

"What's important here," Privek told the group over their headsets, "is that these people are dangerous. No matter how harmless any individual might seem, they all need to be contained. Our methods aren't foolproof, but should give us enough time with each of them safely under control to at least find out if they can be reasoned with."

"What about my Will? What if he's there?" Jasmine's legs bounced nervously and her empty hands fidgeted.

"Yes, there may be a few innocent bystanders among them, so be careful. Brewer's husband went missing with her, for one. There may be others we don't know about. We assume they've all been brainwashed, so don't be surprised if they don't want to come quietly, just be careful not to hurt them. Use only tasers on anyone who doesn't have the eyes, and when in doubt. Alpha Leader is in charge on the ground. We'll be dropping you a mile out from the property to avoid detection."

"Are we sure they're really there?" Dianna sat placidly, her dark face smooth and neutral.

"Yes. Camellia is already on site. She arrived when Mitchell and a few others came back earlier today."

Maisie didn't want to do this at all. Not even a little. Did anyone care? No. This had to be done. They had no other choice. The footage from Hill and the pictures from that cave horrified her enough to throw up. These people had no decency or empathy. That broken infant haunted her nightmares, and she'd only seen a picture of it. How could anyone live with himself after *doing* that?

The worst part seemed to be the idea they could stand up to that kind of firepower. Beyond the babies and kids, these monsters had taken out squads of armed men. The second helicopter held ten SWAT guys from Homeland Security. She thought they'd need ten thousand to have a chance. Privek said the element of surprise, combined with tranq guns and tasers, would be enough.

The gun still felt awkward in her hands, even after two weeks of training with it. The barrel held one shot at a time, and used the four darts strapped to her hip, plus the one already loaded. She'd practiced reloading it until she could do it in five seconds. Everyone else here had done the same except Jasmine. She'd be a squirrel the whole time, and seemed flighty enough that a gun in her hands would probably be a bad idea anyway. At least Liam and Paul looked as awkward with it as she did. Everyone else seemed fine with it.

They landed on a two lane road surrounded by miles and miles of farmland. She snapped off her headset and climbed out behind Raymond to look around. A pinprick of light shone in the distance, but someone pointed in the opposite direction. That way lay a dark splotch of doom, the jagged shapes of giant trees hinted at by the starlight.

She'd been given flares, a flashlight, carabiners, zipties, a lighter, and twenty other things that fit into the tac vest she had to wear to mark herself as 'friendly'. Straightening it gave her something to do with her hands besides awkwardly fondling the gun while waiting for someone to tell her what to do.

Alpha Leader gestured for everyone to gather around while the two helicopters lifted off again. He took a knee in the center and waited for the noise to die away. "Okay, everyone, this is it. We all know what we're in for. Hopefully, they'll all be asleep, but if they aren't, it's their home base, so they shouldn't want to blow it up. Moore," he pointed to Liam, "you stay with Alpha Seven. You'll hang back, but not so far you can't do anything. O'Malley," he pointed to Chelsea, the girl with giant, feathery angel wings, "and Jackson," he pointed to Dianna, who could control the wind, "go in topside, in case anyone is overhead or on the roof. The skies are up to you. The rest of you stay with me, say something if you see something or have any brilliant ideas. Stealth is our friend here. If you can't hack it, move to the back."

Like everyone else, Maisie nodded and stepped away. She took a deep breath and gulped. No longer did she have one more day to train, one more day to think about it, one more day to hope someone else would take care of this for her. Air whipped around as Chelsea's wings beat to get her off the ground and Dianna summoned up the wind to pull her into the sky. Maisie's hands itched. She wanted to get this over with, and also wanted to stay here forever.

Alpha Leader conferred with his men, then he clapped loud enough to startle her. She jumped, her heart racing, and covered her face, wishing she could be doing hula with Rob grabbing her ass instead. If she wanted to avoid getting hurt though, she needed to get a grip and pay attention.

They kicked into an easy jog along the side of the road, gear jangling and her hands finding the gun to keep it from shooting her own foot. "I, um, should be able to get us across anything out in the open," she said uncertainly. The earpiece didn't have a microphone stick going to her mouth, and she felt self-conscious talking without knowing for sure she'd be heard.

"Don't worry," Liam said, patting her shoulder from behind. "If one of them starts trying to hurt you, just pop away to behind Beller. I'll certainly be hiding behind him if I need to."

Raymond chuckled. "Yeah, you can hide behind me and my shield, I don't mind." The muscular black man made the metal shape appear on his arm, in its kite shield form. All the times she'd seen it before, it had been a drab gray color. This time, he'd made it so black it almost sucked light in. She knew it could be as big as a ten foot square and as small as a six inch circle.

"You should be trying to herd them toward me." Brian sounded much more nervous than he looked. His voice quavered, yet his feet moved with rock-solid surety. "Especially Westbrook. I can take what he can dish out."

"I'll do what I can," Paul broke in, "but if any of the rest of them have closed-off minds like Cant or chaotic ones like Mitchell, I won't be much help. I might be able to distract them, but that's about it." From the way he moved, he desperately wanted to holster his gun-thing. The weapons came only with a clip for their vest so they couldn't fall and be lost. Their trainer had told them to avoid doing that, as the stupid things could accidentally go off. Whoever designed it needed a swift kick in the rear for that one.

Kevin stayed quiet, which made sense. He could turn invisible, and it seemed to extend to his personality. Jasmine made excited chirpy noises as she bounced along, her ponytail bobbing and swishing.

Maisie nodded to all the chatter, not sure how to respond other than to hope they didn't all die tonight. "Um, Alpha Leader?" Referring to a human being like that made her feel stupid. "Can you run over the goals part again?" She wanted to remind him that until a few weeks ago, dodging flowers when they fell off the costumes had been one of her biggest problems.

"Sure." He didn't sound annoyed, but had a right to be. These guys normally dealt with trained operatives, not random kids with superpowers. "Goal one is to find the house and re-acquire Androvitch. Goal two is to gain stealth entry into the building. Goal three is to acquire all twenty-four targets without harming an unknown number of civilians. Lethal force is not sanctioned without imminent threat."

"Thanks."

"It's normal to be nervous about something like this." At least Alpha Leader wasn't a dick. He also didn't push them too hard, setting a pace they could all keep up with. It took about ten minutes to reach the driveway, where Camellia stood up, her camouflage fading away.

She took an earpiece from Alpha Two and tucked her phone away in a pocket. "I haven't been able to check out the whole property, but I'm pretty sure there are only two buildings. The farmhouse is where most of them spend their time and live. The barn has two guys living in it, one of us and his boyfriend. I get the impression that one is some kind of inventor—he tinkers with stuff a lot. The farmhouse is big, it's been expanded from its original size. Two doors, one in front, one in the back. Also, plenty of windows. Each bedroom has a window, and the kitchen and their big common room. The basement has casement windows, too."

One of the other Alphas—Maisie hadn't managed to learn all their voices yet—asked, "What're they using the basement for?"

"Storage, so far as I can tell. No one living down there."

"Sounds like a possible entry point," Alpha Leader said. "Alpha Three and Four, you're on it, take Androvitch. Five, Six, and Astrid, target the barn. Subdue, wrap up, and rejoin. Two and Nine with Beller, check the front door. Ten with me on the back door. Arralt, pick a spot you like not too far from the building, and everyone else work on a funnel to get them to him. "

Maisie nodded even though no one would see it and tried to think of how she could help with 'funneling'. Nothing came to mind. In fact, she thought she'd be much more useful trying to get inside. "Alpha Leader, it's Polape. If I can look in through a window, I can throw a portal inside."

"Hm. Alright, new plan. Five, Six, and Astrid, still on the barn. Three and Four, spike the back door as quietly as you can, then join Arralt with Two. Put yourself in the line of fire for the front door, but try to be out of sight from inside. The rest of us are going in through the basement. Stealth is highest priority. If they wake up and start fighting back, everyone gets out as quick as you can. We have orders not to kill, they don't."

"Permission to set annoyance traps?" a different Alpha asked.

"Granted, but keep them away from the door. If we've got to run out, we need to not trip them."

"Understood."

"It's Chelsea. Um, O'Malley, I mean. We've done a sweep of the whole property. There doesn't appear to be anyone outside. They've got animals, though. We saw some chickens and goats. We're over the house now, and can't see anyone."

"Good work, O'Malley. Keep your eyes open and assist as needed. Jackson, do what you can to pick up anyone who comes out through anything other than the front door, or if Arralt and Pearson look like they're getting overwhelmed."

"Yeah, okay," Dianna said. She sounded annoyed, maybe bored.

Lined by a row of stately trees with a wild tangle of younger trees, shrubs, and grasses beyond it, the driveway kept going and going and going. Isolated and overgrown, this property seemed perfect for this purpose. From the highway, no one would expect to find people living here, other than maybe rural hillbillies best left undisturbed.

The driveway ended at a wide empty space with the ground churned up. Alphas shone flashlights around to reveal a bunch of cars and vans parked in a line in front of the one-story house. It appeared normal from the front, with a small porch and dark windows. Camellia's description seemed off-base.

Alpha Leader held up an arm before they crossed the open space. Everyone halted. Paul doubled over to catch his breath. Everyone else, including Maisie, seemed fine. "Two, this is a good place to set up. Seven, stay a good thirty feet back or so. Androvitch, where's the barn?"

Camellia pointed off to the right. "There's a lot of tarps. The two men are in a converted horse stall. And probably naked."

"Let's all go that way," Alpha Leader said quietly, using another hand gesture to get everyone moving. "Lights on the ground, people."

Maisie figured the instruction had been intended for her and pointed her flashlight down. She paid close attention to the ground, avoiding dead leaves and twigs, and small rocks that wanted to trip her.

"If I'm needed, someone will have to tell me," Liam said. "I won't see anything in this."

"Anyone who needs medical, either get yourself there or call 'Medic' and give your position. Whoever's closest goes to pull them to Moore. We don't want to expose him if we can help it."

"From the bottom of my heart, Alpha Leader, I sincerely appreciate that."

Alpha Leader snorted. "No more chatter."

With that, the earpiece in Maisie's ear went silent and they padded across the way to find a window. The house extended much farther than she expected, and this wall had to be new construction. Big, leafy shrubs grew next to it, which confused her. Plants couldn't grow that fast and they hadn't been cut back on the one side. How did they get the shrubs to grow this big this close to what were obviously new outer walls? With flowers.

Someone took the time to get these bushes blooming with pretty flowers. She didn't expect to see flowers. Maybe creepy weird flowers, or wild ones growing wherever. She mostly only knew Hawaiian flowers, so she couldn't say what kind these might be, but she liked them. The delicate pink and white ruffly petals reminded her of the wads of jasmine her aunt grew.

Seeing that made her wonder how much of what Privek told them was really true, and how much he finessed to manipulate them. Surely, he couldn't lie to Paul, though. Paul could poke through people's minds and see their thoughts. Unless Privek didn't know the whole story. They could be pawns and never know it.

Privek had rescued her personally from the men who abducted her in Honolulu. Since she woke up to his face, she hadn't come across any reason to doubt him. The video of what happened at Hill Air Force Base had cemented her trust.

Of course, demented freaks could like flowers. No rule forbade that. Maisie shook off her confusion. Distractions could get someone killed here. Halfway around the side, the barn guys peeled off to handle that and Maisie saw the first window. "Alpha Leader," she whispered, "window." Her attention on the pane of glass, she laid flat on the ground to get a look inside.

Shining her flashlight into the darkness, Maisie saw nothing special:

shelves, baskets, and a washing machine. One washer for this many people almost seemed criminal. Satisfied it had plenty of space, though, she flicked the fingers of her right hand out, causing a swirling blue oval to spring into existence on the nearest wall she could see. She stood up, brushed herself off, and flicked her left hand out, an orange oval appearing on the wall in front of them. Instead of swirling orange and black in the middle, it offered a view into the dark basement, through the blue oval.

Wordlessly, Alpha Leader hopped through. The rest of the Alphas followed him, then the rest of them. They didn't have designations. She didn't want one. It would, however, make referring to them collectively less weird. So far, in her head, she called them all 'freaks'. Some of them seemed like the type to take offense at that, so she never said it out loud.

"We're in," Alpha Leader muttered.

Maisie pulled the blue portal back into her right hand, leaving the orange one in case she needed a quick exit. It made a soft metallic 'whum' noise that cycled endlessly like a sine wave, only noticeable within a foot or so. In fact, she suspected the noise might actually only be in her head. At some point, they'd all be able to discuss their powers together and figure out those sorts of details. To this point, Privek and Alpha Leader had kept them training too hard for that.

Alpha Leader lead the team up the stairs. "Fourteen of us, at least twenty-six of them. Split up and take different doors. Dose and move on. Say something if you need help or one gets away."

Maisie gulped and hoped she didn't get into trouble here. If it came to a fight, she'd lose. Paul tapped her on the shoulder. She turned to see him tap his forehead, then reach over and tap hers. She blinked blankly at him, having no idea what he meant by that. For good measure, since he didn't seem to be getting her confusion, she shrugged.

"I can speak directly into your mind. Is that okay?"

Maisie squeaked with surprise, then clapped a hand over her mouth.

"What happened?" Alpha Leader asked.

"Nothing," Maisie hissed, embarrassed. "Stubbed my toe." She saw him turn and glare at her, then heard him sigh and move on.

"Sorry. I have no idea how to do that more gently."

Staring at Paul, Maisie gulped again and nodded. *"Do I have to do something special?"*

"No, just think what you want to say to me. I don't think I can do this with more than one person at a time, though. You just seemed really nervous, so I thought maybe it would help if you had someone to talk to."

"Uh, thanks. Yeah, this is really a thing, and I'm really scared I'm going to screw it up."

"Me too, actually. I really wish we didn't have to have these gun things."

She agreed, and didn't need to coherently say so for him to get it. But they had more important things to worry about. Alpha Leader turned up a hallway and gestured for the group to split up. Maisie found herself at the end of the line, so she went the other way. Alpha Nine assigned her to a door by pointing. He gave Paul the next door up and sent her some wordless encouragement, which she needed.

Her hand on the knob, she turned it as slowly as she could to avoid making a noise, then inched it open. She found a tiny little bedroom, the floor space only enough to swing the door open. The bed took up most of the room, along with a dresser and small table. A second door inside suggested a closet. The most important thing in the room, though, was the man asleep on the bed. She knew him immediately, recognizing him from the video. Out of all these people, she had to be the one to get Mitchell.

One of the dangerous ones. He'd killed people. Lots of people. Privek had said he might be indestructible.

"I'm scared I'll mess this up."

"Do it fast. Don't hesitate, just do it. It'll be okay."

Maisie lifted the awkward gun and crept into the room. A light breeze tumbled in through the open window and stirred the half-drawn curtains. The screen looked battered; maybe it was old, or maybe he beat on it like a wild animal.

She could do this. So long as he didn't wake up before the drug took effect, he couldn't do anything to her. Pointing her gun at his chest, she took a deep breath to try to calm her stomach. It didn't work. Fine. She just needed to do it, like Paul said.

In her ear, voices announced the assault had begun in earnest. The barn was secure, one subject down, one tased and tied up. One down here, two down there, another one somewhere else. All of it startled her. She shot the gun. It made a little pfft sound and the dart thumped into his chest. Mitchell's eyes snapped open and darted around wildly.

She stared into his confused, frightened icy blue eyes and saw her own. She'd just shot her brother. Her hands shook. Bile threatened to crawl up her throat.

His mouth opened and he made a confused, gurgling noise instead of words. He thrashed around, maybe trying to sit up.

Stumbling away from him, her fingers fumbled to reload the gun, snatching the next dart and shoving it into the chamber. Her leg bumped into the table and she dropped the gun. It went off and shattered against the floor, splashing clear, viscous liquid onto her shoe.

Covering her face in embarrassment and horror, she tried to block out the sounds coming from the bed. Because it sounded like pain, like despair, like death. "Mitchell is down," she croaked.

Someone male swore violently into her ear. Then she heard the loudest noise imaginable, a scream that filled her whole being with terror and agony, and threatened to deafen her. Pawing at her ear, she yanked the device out and dropped it so she could clap her hands over her ears.

CHAPTER 16

The impact woke him. By the time he understood what was happening, the drug had already been delivered into his body. All of Bobby's will focused on getting as many dragons away as he could. They resisted, wanting to sleep and stay put. He kept pushing, throwing everything he had at them. At least one had to be able to get away.

One little dragon crawled sluggishly off his foot, taking the small toe as the drug surged through his system. The edges of his vision blurred, pulling him down into unconsciousness. With one last, desperate effort, he tossed his mind into that one dragon.

It looked around, trying to understand what had happened. A girl in SWAT gear stood over him with a weird-looking gun, then she backed up, her face screwed up in panic. She reloaded her gun with a dart and it went off, hitting the floor.

Owen's super-voice rang out. The girl pulled something out of her ear and dropped it. Her eyes screwed shut and her hands covered her ears. Somehow filtered or muted by the dragon, Bobby found the noise a nuisance. Elsewhere in the house, he heard shouting voices.

The dragon dove to the floor and grabbed the thing she dropped, then flew out of the room. All kinds of people in the same tactical gear filled the house. Lily's door hung open and he wanted to go check on her and Sebastian.

Everyone's doors hung open, he noticed. A man stepped out of Alice's, his next door neighbor, holding his ears. Bobby caught sight of the guy's eyes and saw his own staring back at him. The sight took him one beat, then another, to register, and he suddenly felt stupid and betrayed. All this time, he'd been trying to save that guy, only to have him come here and assault them.

Owen's voice stopped, maybe because of a dart to the chest. Bobby heard a familiar squeal in the sudden silence. "Will! I knew you'd be here!"

Now he had no idea what to think. Jasmine came to assault the farm? He needed to find Stephen. His only recourse here would be killing people, and he had no desire to harm any of them. Not yet. Not until he understood all of this.

It would take him about an hour to get to Denver, then…he'd have to find one girl named Kris, or some variation of it. Stephen hadn't even told him which part of Denver she lived in. For all he knew, her place could be in one of the suburbs, and he had no last name to search for.

No, that was stupid. Stephen would come back before dawn to catch some sleep here. Bobby could wait outside and intercept him before he reached the house, or be here if these people all left by then. That option sucked. It also happened to be the best one available with his body down for the count.

The dragon flitted through the house, darting from hiding spot to hiding spot in a desperate dash to avoid being seen. So long as no one knew he'd gotten one dragon free, he could accomplish something. He could follow them back to their base and free everyone and wreak all kinds of havoc there.

Jayce had managed to get up and change his flesh to steel. The big man roared with defiance and threw a person across the room while darts smashed into him. They'd have a heckuva time putting him down, if they figured out some way to do it.

Bobby would've given a lot to be able to tell Jayce that he had a dragon free, and no matter what, he'd come for them. But he couldn't do anything of the kind without giving himself away. Now he heard Sebastian screaming for his momma, then saw a guy in tac gear carrying the boy as he reached back for Lily. The sight crushed a piece of him. How could a man do that to a little boy? He wanted to do horrible things to that man and only didn't because he knew these men were just following orders.

Privek. He did this. Bobby and Stephen would find him and eat him for breakfast. This time, they'd take that sonofabitch to some hellhole, throw him in, and beat the shit out of him until he told them everything. Or maybe they'd tie him up and do obscene things to him until he begged to die. Or something. No matter what, he'd suffer.

The dragon found a perch in a tall tree and watched, even though it hurt to not be able to do anything about it. Sebastian wailed as the guy carried him away from the house. Jayce burst out of the house and tripped on something as he charged after that guy. Something Bobby couldn't make out in the darkness smashed him to the ground and kept him from getting up again.

Through the earpiece in the dragon's claws, he finally heard voices again.

"This is Alpha Leader. Is anyone back on the channel yet?"

"Nine here, with Polape. She lost her earpiece, but she's fine. This section is cleared."

"Seven here, no issues. Mezilis and the civvie are here with me and Moore."

"Two reporting in. Eight needs a medic, so does Androvitch. We're in the second wing. Need backup."

"Ten on my way."

"Four on my way."

"Party on Two's Six."

"Three here, I've got the kid. He's not calming down. Don't suppose one you is good with toddlers?"

"Suck it up, Three." He recognized Alpha Leader's voice again.

"Everything topside is good." This voice didn't identify itself, but was notable for being female.

"I have my Will!"

"We're all very happy for you, Jasmine." This one spoke through gritted teeth, under serious strain. "Westbrook is contained out here, but he's still putting up a hell of a fight. Paul, get your mindfuck on already."

"I'm trying! He's resisting me."

The strained voice spoke again. "Maybe we should just call him fucking Superman."

"Jesus," Alpha Leader grunted, "anybody got a sledgehammer?"

"I can help if you let him go, Brian." Another female voice spoke. Bobby saw something dropping out of the sky to land gently next to Jayce. So, they had people who could fly. How many of the others did they have on this raid? All eleven? What did Privek tell them?

"Okay, on three, I'm letting him go. One, two, three." For three seconds, he heard nothing over the earpiece. He watched while Jayce, lit up by several flashlights, struggled to push himself up, his face twisted in a rage unlike anything Bobby ever saw him wearing before. He growled and it grew into a roar. Finally, his expression went slack and he slumped to the ground. His skin shimmered to normal flesh tone.

"Holy fucking Christ. Westbrook is down." Someone walked up and shot him with a dart. "And now contained."

"That's that, then," Alpha Leader said. "If anyone else is resisting, they're doing it by hiding and not fighting. Police these bodies outside by Seven for pickup. Seven, keep a count, we need to know if we missed anyone. Nine, get Polape to set us up with a shorter walk."

Bobby flew farther away and wanted to ditch the earpiece. Watching and listening to this hurt enough that he questioned his decision not to kill anyone. The dragon hefted the earbud to toss it for distance so he could stop hearing the awful words.

He stopped it. If they mentioned anything that could help him, he needed to hear it. Not only that, but Stephen might be able to use it against them. Settling on a branch out of sight, he resigned himself to monitoring the cleanup.

They chattered about hoofing bodies, some of which happened to be naked. At least a few demanded they be covered with blankets, and the Alpha Leader agreed. They rooted through Greg's stuff, taking anything that seemed worth the effort. No one realized what his generator did though, and they left it running.

Eventually, they counted their victims. They had twenty-two 'targets', three civilians, and Sebastian. No one knew how to categorize the little boy. That meant someone else besides Stephen was still loose. Only a few got identified by name, so going by what he'd heard and seen, it couldn't be Jayce, Alice, Ai, Greg, Owen, Lily, or Lizzie. Given the quiet, he figured it wouldn't be Dan either. Someone had been able to hide, like Lisa and Sam could.

"Helicopters are inbound," he heard Alpha leader announce. "That means we're done with the tac channel. Alpha Two, police up the earbuds."

"What about those two missing targets?"

"One of them is Cant, he's probably off hunting. Unless he doesn't live here, he'll be back at some point. The file said he's averse to sunlight, so it'll probably be by dawn. So long as you tag him before he gets close, there shouldn't be any problems. No armored skin or anything like that in the file. The other one, we can't confirm the identity of without pictures to compare to our bundles."

"Orders, Boss?"

"Nine, Ten, stay behind and grab Cant when he returns. We'll have a bird standing by, waiting for your call. Just in case it goes sideways, Arralt, stay with them. See if you can find our mystery number twenty-four, but don't sweat it. Probably not here, might even be off on their own."

"Understood."

Bobby watched them all hand in their earbuds. Helicopters took his family away. He wished he couldn't see how stupid it would be to fly into the engines and blow one up. He wished he could find Privek right this minute and rip him apart. Most of all, he wished Stephen had been around to hear all of that so he wouldn't have to find a way to explain it through a dragon, without words.

This shouldn't have happened. They relied on secrecy for security, when they should have done something active to make the place safe. Was it the trip to Alamogordo, or Stephen's forays into Denver, or Kaitlin using her money? Who knew, and who cared? They should've been paranoid. They should've expected this to happen eventually and planned for it. Their priorities had been all wrong. Knowing changed nothing right now.

Dropping the earbud as useless now, he flew a circuit of the property, checking for anyone who might have hunkered down on the edges or chosen to sleep outside tonight. He saw goats and chickens, but no people.

Tony could've turned himself into a plant and be hiding in plain sight. Sam could be in the house wiring, Lisa could be in her pocket, Violet could have flown somewhere, John could have encased himself in a tree. He held onto hope that he'd be able to find another ally after Stephen took care of Nine, Ten, and Arralt.

When he returned to the farmhouse, he saw the three men left behind. Two of them gave off a military vibe as they crouched on the ground, futzing with something. That made the other one Arralt, a brother willing to work for Privek for some reason. He scribbled license plate numbers on a notepad.

That girl who shot Bobby seemed so scared and unwilling. He wondered what story Privek spewed to get them all to believe they needed to come here, wreck the house, and tie up their brothers and sisters like dogs. Did he have some leverage over them, like blackmail? Did he learn from the mistakes with him and Jayce and Ai and Alice to manipulate those others better?

Avoiding the three men, Bobby slipped back inside the house and flew from room to room. The dragon let out a soft trill wherever he thought the men outside might not overhear, hoping to find someone tucked away. It wound up in Lily's room, and he had to turn away to get Sebastian's screams to stop echoing in his head.

The place had been wrecked. They'd smashed furniture, ripped down doors, and punched giant holes in the walls. Bobby saw broken picture frames in bedrooms. Plants lay in piles of dirt, surrounded by shards of pottery. Tiana's cat had been shot with a dart that had ripped fatally through its small body, staining the ground with its blood.

Finally, a closet door opened in response to his trill. Kaitlin stuck her tinfoil-wrapped head out, clutching her laptop to her chest "Is it safe?" she whispered, peering around.

He swooped in and wished he could hug her. The dragon sat on her knee and held up three claws. Asking about the tinfoil seemed too hard, so he ignored it.

"There are three of us, or three of them?"

Both questions technically had the same answer. He nodded. In an attempt to explain to her about Stephen, the dragon put two claws up by its mouth like fangs, doing its best Dracula impersonation.

"Stephen wasn't here, he's off with his girlfriend?" The dragon nodded. "Is that you in there, Bobby?" Nod. "Because they got you?" Nod. "And there are three of them outside waiting for Stephen to come back?" Nod. "Well, shit." She rubbed her forehead. "We're kind of fucked." Nod. "Thanks for agreeing," she said sarcastically. "I feel so much better now."

The dragon put up the claw-fangs again, pointed to itself, then pointed outside. Kaitlin nodded. "Yeah, good idea. You go wait for Stephen, intercept him. I can keep myself clear." She held out a finger to rub the dragon's belly, which it liked more than he expected it to. "Sorry I couldn't save anyone else. I didn't understand what I was seeing until it was too late."

Hoping she wouldn't spend much time beating herself up over that, he patted her knee and took off. She deserved zero blame for any of this. He, on the other hand, needed to have his ass kicked. That trip down to White Sands had to be the way they found the farmhouse. The timing hit too close for coincidence. Maybe someone found the car while Jayce had been banging that park ranger and slipped some...thing... Actually, now that he thought about it, the trunk had popped open randomly when they picked Sam up. Considering their varied abilities, one of them could've hit the release while they were all distracted and jumped in or thrown in a tracking device.

The assault on the farm had been his fault. Chicago had been his idea. Afghanistan had been his call. Albuquerque had been his plan. Everyone else suffered for it. Sebastian's screams echoed in his head again, and some part of his mind helpfully replayed the memory of seeing him hauled away, terrified.

This hiding crap ended now. No matter how it fell out when they got free, there would be no more hiding, no more huddling together for anything other than kinship and camaraderie. He'd stand up and tell the whole world what he could do and how little he cared what they thought about it. The bunch of them would do what they wanted to do, not what other people wanted them to do.

Perched in a tree again, the dragon sat and stared out at the sky, expecting Stephen to come from the southwest. He'd fly in a straight line, and should pass by this point to reach the house. Hopefully, he actually would come back this morning. If they all had to wait a couple of days while he got laid and fed a few times, there might be a problem.

Trying avoid thinking, Bobby dozed and wondered about the condition of his body. Would they try to 'reason' with him, or judge him too dangerous and unreasonable to bother? If he hadn't managed to get a dragon off, they could've set him up to be drugged into unconsciousness for the rest of his life. Finding that depressing, he forced himself to think about something else.

His mind latched onto Will, the one person here whose situation seemed weirder than his own. He could easily imagine how they got Jasmine confused enough to actually believe she was doing the right thing. Now they'd have to convince Will, a guy smart enough to become a genuine veterinarian. Either that, or they'd have to tread a line between threats and action to get him to play along without alienating Jasmine.

That led him to wondering about the others. Arralt seemed to think he'd picked the right side. That girl in Bobby's room seemed conflicted about hurting him, so they hadn't been turned into assassins or monsters. Unlike himself, a tiny voice reminded him. Stephen probably had the right of it: nothing was as simple as he wanted it to be.

With dawn, Bobby saw a dark spot appear in the sky. The dragon leaped into the air to intercept him. Fortunately, Stephen happened to be the one person who, upon being accosted by a single dragon, knew to accept it and start asking simple questions.

He looked good, well fed and sated. Bobby caught up with him near the edge of their property. The vampire had already pulled his gloves on and settled his balaclava into place. "One dragon? Bobby, are you in there?" Nod. "Something happened, then." Nod. "Are you in there because your body is in trouble?" Nod. "Is this all an epic joke you're helping to play on me as penance for our trip?"

Stunned and stung by the accusation, it took Bobby a few seconds to come up with an answer. The dragon shook its head fervently.

Stephen snorted. "Sure, right. I believe you." Rolling his eyes as he turned to face away from the sun, he continued at full speed to the farm-house.

Unwilling to give up, the dragon grabbed his coat and clung, chirping madly to get his attention. Dammit, if he could just talk!

"Cut it out, Bobby, seriously. I get they're all pissed at us, but you're trying too hard." He landed in the clearing in front of the house.

Bobby saw a dart thump into the vampire's chest, a few inches away from the dragon. The dragon trilled out the curses he wanted to shout and he let go to watch Stephen blink stupidly at the dart, drop to his knees, and collapse.

Something wrapped around the dragon, encasing Bobby in a world of distorted light. It pressed close, then it crushed him and everything went black.

Epilogue – Brian

"Damn, I didn't mean to crunch it." Brian pulled his hand back. It returned to normal from its liquid state with a smashed dragon in his palm. "I hope that didn't kill him."

"Call it in, Ten." Nine nudged Cant with a boot.

Ten pulled out his phone and made the call. "Alpha Base, this is Alpha Ten, we have Cant."

Poking the little metal corpse, Brian sighed. "Ask them who the last missing one is, and if Mitchell is okay. I just crunched one of his dragons."

Ten relayed the questions for him while Nine used zipties to secure Cant. Ending the call, Ten said, "Base reports Mitchell's vitals are clear. The last one is Kaitlin Tremont, abilities unknown. None of the captures are awake yet to interrogate. Orders are to sweep the house and property one more time, then call for pickup. Here's a picture. She's cute."

Brian rolled his eyes. All the girls were cute, or hot, or had plenty of potential. "I'll go look through the woods. You guys check the house."

"Copy that." Nine dragged Cant into the shade and left him by a tree trunk. "Watch your six."

"Yeah, you too." Brian's entire body liquefied, becoming a mass of water with an outer membrane stronger than steel. Someday, he wanted to understand how what they could all do didn't violate every law of physics.

For now, he sloshed through the trees and shrubs faster than a person could run, his ability to see somehow spread across his entire outer skin. Everything about his superpower was weird, much like Mitchell's. He really hoped the guy was actually okay, because out of all of them, he really wanted to talk to Mitchell. About being this level of crazy weird, mostly.

Books by Lee French

The Maze Beset Trilogy
Dragons In Pieces
Dragons In Chains
Dragons In Flight

Fantasy in the Ilauris setting
Damsel In Distress
Shadow & Spice (short story)

The Greatest Sin series
(co-authored with Erik Kort)
The Fallen
Harbinger

About the Author

Lee French lives in Olympia, WA with two kids, two bicycles, and too much stuff. She is an avid gamer and active member of the Myth-Weavers online RPG community, where she is known for her fondness for Angry Ninja Squirrels of Doom. In addition to spending much time there, she also trains year-round for the one-week of glorious madness that is RAGBRAI, has a nice flower garden with one dragon and absolutely no lawn gnomes, and tries in vain every year to grow vegetables that don't get devoured by neighborhood wildlife.

She is an active member of the Northwest Independent Writers Association, the Pacific Northwest Writers Association, and the Olympia Area Writers Coop, as well as being one of two Municipal Liaisons for the NaNoWriMo Olympia region.

Thanks for reading! If you enjoyed this book, please take a minute to review it on Goodreads and wherever you buy your books.

www.authorleefrench.com

21442480R00131

Made in the USA
Middletown, DE
30 June 2015